Three Trees began as a whisper a[...] previous book, *Eden's Blueprint*. [...] seemed to open more curiosity i[...] of our loving Designer, revealing new understandings of how we were designed to love and be loved. You will find your spirit connecting with the characters as Matt gives them real emotions and reactions to their life experiences. As you are drawn into the story, I would encourage you to give yourself permission to get curious and explore the Designer's plan for the world He created through this expansion on long-told stories of Adam, Eve, and their family.

Trish Beckenham
Greater Things International
www.greaterthingsinternational.com

I don't think there has ever been a greater need than right now for new parables to help us contextualize the Bible in our modern day. What Matt has done through this rich narrative, divinely rooted in scripture, allows us to walk directly into the heart of the Father. As we follow the characters and their time with the Designer, we are finding ourselves sitting at the table, feasting on the revelations of this fictional masterpiece. Matt's ability to take biblical themes and express them through his own life and journey, shapes and forms characters that come off of the pages and into our own stories. Not only are the characters relatable but as they face challenges and grow in their relationships towards one another and their Creator, so do we.

Matt's creative approach to re-imagining the story of Adam and Eve and their departure from Eden invites us into a new world of thought-provoking concepts and perspectives. Not only does he open up new conversations within the Old Testament, but he craftily weaves in fundamental truths from the New Testament as well. This gives us a fresh, comprehensive approach to the scripture that will leave a legacy in the hearts of every reader that comes across its path.

Jessie DeCorsey
Artist
jessiedecorsey.com

Three Trees by Matt Beckenham is not just a book—it is a profound encounter with Love Himself. It is said that a book has true impact when the reader has to put it down numerous times just to process the depths of what was just read. *Three Trees* was just that for us! Matt's use of creative license, in obvious partnership with the Holy Spirit, has produced an allegory that we believe will have a weighty impact on anyone who reads it. The depiction of the Fall, the seeing Eagle and his friend Wisdom, as well as the story of Cain and Abel, gives precious insight into the heart of the Father and His great mercy and grace for His beloved creation. It drives the reader to long for greater depths of friendship with our great "Designer." This book is a tool to bring awakening to the vast expanses of His love and His heartbeat.

Carston and Mandy Woodhouse
Outrageous Hope
www.mandywoodhouseoutrageoushope.com/carstonandmandy

This book swoons you. It is not so much the words and phrases as it is the "voice" in the text that calls you on, calling you deeper and deeper into understanding and wonder, like these sentences, "When the Designer speaks of love, I feel the atmosphere around me shimmer. I know I do not hear just words; I am actually feeling a power that creates and restores." A beautiful and powerful story.

Michael Henderson
Artist & Writer
www.michaeljameshenderson.com.au

I loved this book, and it really touched my heart. I had many genuine encounters with the Father, and I still feel Him talking to me about many things the book stirred in me. I love the imagery and different angles of how Matt approaches the story of The Fall, Cain, and Abel.

Rob Feeney
Senior Leader Gracepoint Christian Church
www.gracepoint.com.au

The prologue and epilogue of *Eden's Blueprint* left me, and I know many others, wanting more. The way in which Matt is able to write a story of fiction soaked in biblical and theological truth leads to a reading experience that is not only enjoyable but potentially transformative for the reader. As you read *Three Trees*, what you see is Matt's heart, his love for Jesus, and his desire for people to know the freedom that God offers poured into the narrative of the Eagle.

My hope is that as you read this book, you will encounter the love of the God who is so well represented in its pages and discover more of how He sees you and desires relationship and partnership with you. May you discover that, like the Eagle, you have wings to fly with your Creator!

Rev'd Carl Smith
Church of England Vicar and Writer, UK

Matt Beckenham writes books that connect the readers to God in such an intimate and stunning way. It challenges stale ideals of God. It awakens parts of your heart that you didn't know were sleeping. This is a book that you could read in a day or linger over each page, allowing it to sink in deep. This is a book that will transform and deeply impact hearts.

Lisa Bruton
Director and founder of Arise Sanctuary
www.lisabruton.com.au

Also by Matt Beckenham

Eden's Blueprint

THREE TREES

MATT BECKENHAM

Illustrated by Jessie DeCorsey

GREATER THINGS
international

Published by Greater Things International
Sydney, New South Wales, Australia
www.greaterthingsinternational.com

First published 2023

 A catalogue record for this
book is available from the
NATIONAL
LIBRARY National Library of Australia
OF AUSTRALIA

ISBN: 978 0 6457868 0 4 (Paperback)
ISBN: 978 0 6457868 1 1 (Hardback)
ISBN: 978 0 6457868 2 8 (ePub)

Cover designed by Jessie DeCorsey
Typeset by Helen Christie
Printed by Ingram Spark

To Trish,

*Thank you for listening, reading, and reviewing every chapter.
Thank you for bringing your unique view of life to this book.*

*Our story is entwined on every page, and I am forever thankful
that you are my Wisdom and you are my Eve.*

ACKNOWLEDGMENTS

Trish Beckenham, Jade Schultz, Kate Johnson, and Jessie DeCorsey, thank you all for your time and patience in helping me get my head around the English language.

Jessie DeCorsey, what can I say? You have helped me wrestle through some of the toughest theological challenges of this story! And then, your creative ability to bring many of these chapters to life takes my breath away. We are so thankful for you and all that you do to help make our dreams a reality.

Winifred (Winnie) DeCorsey (age 6), thank you so much for your artwork of the eagle, Wisdom! As soon as I saw your picture, I knew it needed to be in this book!

Roma Waterman! Thank you so much for being willing to write the foreword. We could not think of a better person to do this for a project like Three Trees.

Lastly, thank you to all who call me "friend." Your love has changed my life for the better and made God a whole lot clearer for me.

FOREWORD

by Roma Waterman

One of the best ways we learn is through stories.

I remember reading that before notated music was invented, melodies and lyrics were passed down by singing songs to the next generation until they were embedded and retained in their minds. Then that generation would sing them to the next, and so on.

The lost art in this method of 'remembering' is that memories become attached in the passing down of melody. Who sang it and where, how old the listener was … all these moments contributed to the powerful imprint left on young ears and hearts as they learned the songs of their forefathers.

I often wonder what it would be like to hear the melodies that once accompanied the Psalms. I wonder about the intonation in David's singing, the movement of notes, the inflection and the emotion, the timbre of his voice, mingled with the words we so often read in our Bibles or roll off our tongues. It gives me a greater picture of Psalm 45:1 that The Message translation so beautifully expresses: *"My heart is stirred by a noble theme as I recite my verses for the king; my tongue is the pen of a skillful writer."*

In the same way, we come alive reading stories passed down to us. Stories have meaning. We are not merely reading facts, statistics, or research (even though, without realizing it, we probably are), but the story takes precedence because it is filled with feeling and emotion. This is because a good story is often about real people with real fears, struggles, joy, pain, life, and hope. We read these stories as if they were our own, subconsciously comparing our own experiences as we read of the lives of others. This makes them so powerful and inevitably also helps us remember what might be facts, figures, and research after all.

For example, as Christians, we might diffuse frankincense and remember the birth of Jesus. We understand the bustling life of ancient Israel when we read about the breaking of bread, the jars of water turned into wine, or the Israelites walking the dusty desert that pulses with heat under a Middle Eastern sun. We know about Jesus by the stories we read and also the stories He told. I love what one of my favorite authors Madeleine L'Engle writes in her beautiful book Walking on Water: Reflections on Faith and Art: *"Jesus was not a theologian. He was God who told stories."*

And thus, we learn theology by story. It is the best way to learn, really. Because we attach our experience of hearing or reading to what would otherwise be static black letters on a crisp, white page. Our experience of the story is just as important as the story itself in bringing enlightenment and transformation to our hearts.

This brings me to the book you have before you now. *Three Trees* is a story to be passed down, imagined, and shared. In one way, it's the Gospel story, but in another, it's our story. Part theology, part imagination, and all heart, Matt has creatively weaved an interpretation that gathers up His perspective from years as a pastor, theologian, and spiritual compass to many. But most importantly, it is written through the lens of an authentic lover of Jesus. It is reminiscent of Christian spirituality books like *The Pilgrim's Progress* or *The Cloud of Unknowing*. He has taken the Bible story perceived through the eyes of an Eagle for a bird's eye perspective of the great love of *The Designer*. Please read this re-imagined story as if you are knowing it for the first time.

A good book won't just answer questions; it will make you ask new ones. May it grow your hunger to read the scriptures with new passion and vigor as further questions arise. Allow it to give you a fresh perspective. Place yourself in the story. It will provide you with a deeper insight as you delve into scripture with new eyes. May it illuminate the truth you may already know

I love Matt's creativity in writing, but more importantly, I love his heart—not just for Jesus and truth, but for others. This book is his offering to God, cathartic to write, and now, just like those songs passed down, it becomes a passed-on story for you. Remember in the reading how you feel and what arises, and allow the imprint of *The Designer* to mark your heart with a new burning for Him. Thank you, Matt, for making decisions that carved a unique and creative path for you to write such a beautiful book!

And to the reader—as this story is passed on to you, read to remember. May you never forget that you are part of a bigger story that is both old, new, and unfolding. One in which Father God planned before the age. No matter where you are in your story, He knew the ending before you even began and had a carefully laid out plan from day one. May *Three Trees* remind you of this truth and give you hope that all will be well—now, always, and forever.

Roma Waterman
Founder HeartSong Prophetic Alliance

"Without love, judgment will usually look like punishment. With love, there is no judgment."

PROLOGUE

Eden is the place of my birth, or should I say my creation. It's a land filled with so much life. I don't remember being a young eagle, and to be truthful, I have no idea how old I am or how many days have passed since that first day sitting with the Designer.

This land the Designer simply called Eden feels beyond description. To be able to understand all that has been created, one must encounter it. From the smallest insect to the greatest mountain, all of it carries the Designer's heart and handiwork. He is in every detail and can be seen in everything He has created, including me.

The mountains here in Eden surpass imagination. They tower up from the ground, and few animals can climb high enough to see all they hold. The tops of these mountains are so high they reach into clouds, and when the clouds aren't hiding their peaks, they reveal the snow that crowns them. They are magnificent to behold.

To fly to the top, I pass over forests of pine and cedar trees. Their scent often beckons me to come and land in them and to breathe deeply of the fresh air that they produce. The animals that roam among them are a wonder to behold. There are so many species here that I find it hard to remember them all. Above the tree line lies whole tussock grass areas that move so beautifully in the wind. I love to sit and watch this happen. There, I can feel the rhythm of His design as I see and feel the subtle changes in the atmosphere around me. Above the tussock, there is very little growth; I think it's too cold for many things to grow in these places.

However, rocky outcrops can be covered in moss, lichen, and the most beautiful tiny wildflowers. Even though these flowers are small, they contain every color imaginable. They are so delicate and yet so full of life. Above them, I get to the snow. It glistens in the bright sunlight. It is cold up here, but it is no less beautiful. When the sun is on the snow for long enough, it melts, providing the most extraordinary waterfalls flowing from the mountains. There are no two the same! They have forged pathways through the crust of the mountains, which end up in beautiful turquoise pools of water that feed the mighty rivers surrounding Eden. I feel I have gone through four different seasons by the time I have flown to the top of these mountains.

I have watched more sunsets and sunrises than I could possibly remember. But each one of them is somehow stunningly memorable. The colors that streak across the sky are unique and beautiful. I often forget all else around me as I sit in awe. I love the Designer's creation!

I love my design! I can soar further than other animals. I have learned to find the thermal winds enabling me to go higher and higher. He has given me eyes to see a tiny movement from a great distance. Not much escapes me. When soaring high on the thermals, I feel the fullness of my design. I feel free to be who I am, go where I wish to, and see all there is to see.

The Designer has created many different types of birds, and they are all so beautiful and perfect in their own way. Many of them have voices and create such melodious songs. When I hear them sing, I can sense the joy of the Designer, and he loves to listen to His creation operating in its design.

Few of those birds can fly where I can reach. I don't know why He created me like this. All I know is that when I'm soaring, well, there are no words to describe all I am experiencing in those moments.

Often when I join the Designer walking through Eden, in the time He loves best, the cool of the evening, He asks me what I have seen. The smile rarely leaves His face as I describe all I have experienced. I know he already knows everything I am describing; He made it! But it brings Him such joy when I share my experience with Him. There was even a time when I said to Him, "You would not believe what I have seen!" I laugh at those words now.

I love to fly close to Him as He walks. I often hear Him saying to himself, "It is good." At first, I thought He was talking to me, but on one of those days, of one of those weeks, of one of those months, of one of those years, I realized He was simply speaking to Himself of the wonder of His own creation, and truly, everything here is good. Everything is working in harmony, and everything is of His design.

Everything works so organically. I watch as pairs of animals become families of animals. I watch as seeds of trees become trees of their own, just by the seed working its way into the ground. There is something about the ground too. Again, it's hard to explain, but I feel alive when I'm sitting on it. It's like the essence of the Designer flows through it, which to me, feels like life and joy flow from it.

CHAPTER 1

My favorite time of day is the dawn. I love watching as the sun moves across all the Designer created. As its warmth touches everything, creation comes alive. I love soaring above it all to watch it come alive. The colors, the scents, the sounds, and the coolness connect my spirit with His creation.

This is my home. Here, I rest in the precision and purpose of my design to be His eyes and ears and report back to Him everything I witness in Eden, His Garden, the beloved blueprint of the Designer himself.

I witnessed when the Designer first created a person in His own image, and it was a wonder to behold. I saw Him form Adam from the dust with His own hands. But when He breathed into Adam, all of creation stood still and held its breath. We all witnessed the first breath of those made in His image.

I remember when the Designer presented each of us to Adam. We all received our names from him that day. He looked each of us in the eye and lovingly spoke our identity over us. It is a fine thing to know who I am.

Oh, but then I witnessed something that stirred my heart. After naming all of us, Adam asked the Designer about his partner; He longed to walk with someone like him. The Designer already knew of his need, and He obviously had a plan to make this happen.

That evening, the Designer put Adam into a deeper sleep than he had ever known. It is impossible to describe how the Designer did it, but He took half of Adam and formed another. Then, as He had before, He breathed into the new one like He did with Adam. When she breathed in and awoke, we all saw that although she was similar, she was different, and she was beautiful. The Designer simply called her Eve.

When Adam awoke, he could not believe what he was seeing. The Designer had taken one and made two, but when they were together, their hearts made them one again. Wherever they went in Eden, they would always be together. The joy they shared affected all of creation. When they laughed, we all laughed. When they spoke, we all listened.

I remember when the Designer told them about the plants in Eden. The wonder on their faces was infectious as they learned about each plant and its unique design. The day the Designer led them through the fruit trees is a day I will never forget. They ate every fruit they saw until they could eat no more. There were oranges, plums, apples, avocados, grapefruit, passionfruit, and mangoes; the list goes on and on. They never tired of returning daily to feast on another fruit they had yet to try.

I was also there the day the Designer showed them the *two trees* in the middle of Eden. The mighty *Tree of Life* stood as the centerpiece of His design. It was easily the largest tree in the garden and was stunning to behold. Its fruit was equally stunning to taste. The Designer told them we all could eat from it whenever they liked. And, with just a bite of this fruit, I would feel life pulsing through every fiber of my body.

There was another *tree* near it. It wasn't nearly as big, and its fruit wasn't nearly as beautiful. The Designer called it *The Tree of Knowledge of Good and Bad.* He told them plainly that this fruit was not to be eaten, or death would result. Every animal knew this as well; although He did not say any such thing to us, we each kept away from its fruit.

And truly, I tell you, Adam and Eve lacked nothing, as they were given everything. The Designer would walk with them every evening while they listened to every word that flowed from Him. All of creation responded at the sound of His voice. As He spoke, we could all feel His love through every word.

That was, until one of those days, in one of those weeks, in one of those months, in one of those years, when everything changed.

Each day in Eden was a gift, another glimpse into the life running through the tree. I was delighted to watch the man and the woman feast on the most treasured fruits. I feasted myself, and as I did, a warmth flowed through and out of me. Each cell within me experienced the love and vibrant life that cascaded from every bite. You see, I know the taste and the pleasure. Day after day, week after week, month after month, and year after year, I watched the man, the woman, and every living thing partake in the purest form of love ever known.

But it was Adam and Eve that I had been commissioned to focus my watch on. I knew them as I knew myself. I watched every path they would take, and I was filled with joy while observing them living in their perfect design, just as they were destined to. But the day everything changed came swiftly, and I could not stop it or save them, and I could not step outside of time and pull them back on track. Their path of choice began to concern me. Over time, their path widened, and then they began to move around differently. Their footsteps moved closer and closer to the *tree* that had not been offered to them.

Each day, they would walk by. I flew closer when they did, but I did not intervene; I just observed. One day, I saw them point at the tree and then continue on. The next day, they stopped at the *tree* and spoke about it. They were wondering what the fruit might taste like, but then they continued on their path. I felt my feathers bristle, a sensation that had never occurred before. Until now, no creature had gone near the *tree*, for we all knew the words spoken to Adam and what would happen if they ate from that *tree*.

During this time, I noticed something strange begin to happen. Each time Adam and Eve walked near the *tree*, all the creatures in Eden became restless. The peace in Eden would start to splinter and bristle, and sometimes a mist would arise as confused murmurs began simmering. It only happened when Adam and Eve neared the *tree*, and things would settle back to peace as they moved away.

There are some days that remain etched in my mind, and this was such a day. One of the animals in Eden that Adam had called a lizard wasn't acting like a lizard. It wasn't making lizard sounds, and all the other lizards began avoiding it. I watched as the strange lizard began lurking near the *Tree of Knowledge of Good and Bad* as though he were hunting for something. He began moving through Eden differently. He steered clear of the *Tree of Life*, and alarm rustled through me as he settled beneath the other *tree*. It was almost as if the atmosphere shifted; Eden became still and moved in slow motion before my eyes.

Eve walked the path alone that day and came upon the *tree*. The lizard appeared to be hoping for this, relying on this separation of the man and the woman. Then suddenly, words like those that only Adam and Eve had spoken came out of its mouth. I saw the sky grow dark and knew I had to move quickly! I had to tell the Designer! He needed to know what was happening under this *tree*!

But before I could take flight to find Him, I became acutely aware of His presence. He was sitting beside me in my watchtower tree, and He was watching as well. My entire being was swirling with unease.

I implored Him, "My Lord, allow me to use the razor-sharp talons you gave me. I will pluck that lizard away from Eve and drop him off a cliff, ending this corruption!"

Gently He spoke to me, "This is Eve's moment. She has been here before; she knows my words, and now she has a choice."

Never had I raised my voice to the Designer, but shrillness screamed out of me as I screeched, "This will affect us all!"

He emphasized to me, "This is Eve's moment."

Aghast, I pleaded with Him, "Allow me to bring the man, Adam, here. Surely he will stop this!"

"No," said my Lord, "I have given Adam my words. He knows them, and today we will see if he trusts them."

The Designer, my Lord, God of the universe, then turned toward me and, looking right into my being, said, "Can you see what is happening to my creation when my words are silenced? Can you feel it in the atmosphere? Can you see the turmoil within the animals? Can you feel it within yourself? You've never felt the feelings flowing through you right now, at this moment."

Every fiber of my being lurched and spilled out as tears seared my feathers.

I cried out, "All this is wasted then, all of it ... the peace, the harmony, the connection, and the love."

"No," He replied, "Nothing is wasted. The worst this strange lizard can do is nothing compared to what my love can do. You are about to see the power of death in all its fullness, but through it, and given time, you will see the infinite power of my love. It is beyond anything and everything a corrupt lizard can offer."

I sat next to my Lord, my Designer, and watched in horror. As Eve took a bite of the fruit, a trickle of crimson ran down her lips and chin. I grieved as I watched Adam move toward them, and as Eve had eaten, so did Adam. The strange lizard's face became distorted by a smug expression in the grave moment the man Adam and the woman Eve realized exactly what they had done.

The lizard cackled and mocked. His laughter over their shame burned their skin as they scrambled for leaves to cover themselves and hide from God. The lizard had tried to hide from God once before, but he quickly found out that there was nowhere he could hide. So that's what he did; that strange, distorted lizard just waited for God to come. And I could see into his soul that when the Designer came, the filthy lizard would gloat.

Rage tore through me. It was something I had never felt before, and its power gripped and terrified me. I could feel myself losing control when the Designer's voice, the voice that soothes and heals, the voice that breathes life and cascades over grief like honey, gently settled me.

He said, "They have eaten the fruit they were told not to. But there is the *Tree of Life,* and it is not broken. It will continue to do all that I planned for it to do. If the strange lizard had been wise, he would have tried to convince Adam and Eve that it should be chopped down or destroyed. But he did not, and he will soon see the error of his thinking."

Perching myself again and settling my wings, even in my nearness to the Designer, I could not help but lament over all I had just witnessed. A feeling of helplessness and uselessness came upon me. My Lord had given me a job to watch over the ones like Him, the ones made in His image, His beloved Adam and Eve, and when all I wanted to do was protect them, rescue them, and prevent them from the gravest decision of their lives, the Designer had not allowed it. It was then that I first knew the wrestle of pride and doubt, and that is when My Lord reached out. He knew my thoughts. He gently placed His hand upon my head and stroked it for a time, and as when He first created me, I relaxed beneath

His touch, His love drawing me back to warmth and wholeness. Then he spoke out the words that shifted the atmosphere again with their beauty.

"You have been given the privilege of watching two of the most powerful forces that exist at work. The first is choice: the ability to choose to be in relationship with me. The second is love. When I get down from this tree and go find my beloved ones, you will see the beginnings of the greatest love story that has ever been known. This time, no strange lizard will be able to stop it."

The Designer looked up at the sky and saw that the sun was setting, the warmth of the day was lifting, and the stars would soon fill the sky with their glittering as the cool of the evening moved through Eden. I knew this was the time of day that He loved the most. It was the time when he would walk in the quiet of the evening with those He created to be in relationship with.

CHAPTER 2

I watched as the Designer climbed out of the tree and walked along His familiar paths. I knew He knew where they were, but He walked as if He didn't. He knew all they had done. He'd watched every moment unfold, yet He was unhurried. It was the cool of the evening, and He so loved walking with them both.

As I sat and watched, I cried. I wept for the choices that were made and for the effect that this choice had on Eden. I cried for Adam and Eve ... they now saw things and knew things they wished they didn't. But most of all, I cried for the Designer. He'd put His best into everything that I could see. Every tree, flower, fruit, mountain, lake, and ocean leaked His glory. It was all good!

The confusion in my spirit was real, and the feelings I sensed were impossible to understand. As I sobbed, I became aware of another presence beside me; Wisdom sat with me. She was everything I was, but she carried something more I needed to hear. I could feel the hope she carried, and I wondered whether it would soothe my aching heart.

She turned to me and asked, "Why are you crying?" I nearly fell out of the tree! I couldn't believe Wisdom was so unaffected by all that had happened. She smiled and said, "Oh, you think this is the end?" I sat and silently wept while nodding my head. I couldn't see another outcome.

So Wisdom said, "Did not the Designer tell you this was the start of the greatest love story?"

Again, through my tears, I nodded. I'd heard Him, but I hadn't understood Him.

Again she smiled and said, "In many years' time, One will come, and you will see the love song in all of its glory. What makes no sense now will make perfect sense then. This One will talk about a seed. He will explain that a seed needs to die in the ground for new life to happen. Then once it has been in the ground for long enough, you will see so much life that this Garden cannot contain it. Eagle, can you now see the seed that I speak of?"

"But when will this happen?" I was pleading now. My heart was broken, and all I could feel was loss. I couldn't see what Wisdom saw, and I couldn't comprehend what she was saying.

Once again, Wisdom smiled at me and said, "Eagle, you have been so faithful, and you have clung to every word He has spoken. You know the Designer's words are life, and you have felt life flow through you every time He speaks. This is now a time to listen and discover the life force that flows from His words again. It is hard, I know, but that does not mean it's impossible. Just listen and hear the Designer's words again."

So my gaze moved then to Eden, and I heard the Designer calling to the man and the woman. He was calling them by name. "Adam, Eve, where are you?" It was then that I realized what Wisdom meant. I could hear the words, but it was what I felt that impacted me. I could feel such extraordinary love. Each word was an invitation to heal and not to hide. Each word was a call to restoration and not destruction. Each word was shifting the atmosphere of Eden again. I could feel life flowing through it again. I could feel order coming back. My soul was soaring, and I wanted to take flight and rejoice.

But this time, it was Wisdom that reached out and stopped me. I was confused because I wanted to fly and declare freedom. Wisdom, though, took hold of me and looked into my eyes, saying, "Watch and listen."

So, I watched, and as I did, I felt the tears start flowing again. Adam and Eve had clothed themselves with fig leaves, and they could not look at the Designer. They were not feeling the life and love I was feeling. There was something else at play here. I had felt this same feeling when the strange lizard started lurking under the *Tree of Knowledge of Good and Bad*. Now here it was again; I could feel hope slipping away. I started screaming for the Designer to tread on the head of the lizard! Again, I wanted to fly down and destroy that strange lizard.

Wisdom once again held me back and said, "It's not the Designer's responsibility to silence the voice of the lizard. For this to be a love story, Adam and Eve need to choose the Designer's voice above all others."

"But Wisdom," I screamed. "They haven't chosen to do that! They're still listening to the lizard!"

Wisdom simply nodded and said, "Yes, but it will not always be so. For now, they will leave Eden and find a new home, and that strange lizard will find out the weight of Eve's heel. But rest assured, the Designer will not leave them, and you will again be charged to watch over them. You will see many things. Some will burden you, and some will make you rejoice. Eden will close for a time, but it will only be for a time. Remember, the seed needs to die before the new life begins."

CHAPTER 3

"Eden will close for a time! Wisdom, what does that even mean?"

Even as I screeched that out, I realized Wisdom no longer sat beside me, and the Designer had taken her place! Initially, I was embarrassed because I had said such things out loud for Him to hear. But His gentle response to me calmed the anxiety flowing through every part of my body.

"Eagle, as I said, there are many things you cannot fully understand right now, but I am asking you to trust me. I've commissioned you to watch and see. Are you willing to do this again for me?"

"Yes, my Lord, I am." So I sat back in my tree and watched what happened next.

What I saw horrified me. I had expected those fig leaves, sown so ridiculously together, would be removed. But what I witnessed, I will never forget. It is etched into my mind, and not for the first time, I wished I had not witnessed what I had seen. The Designer climbed down from the tree and killed some of His creation to replace the fig leaves.

My heart is broken. It was the first time I had witnessed death, and I was lost for words.

I looked around at Eden, and its beauty had faded a little for me. I could still see everything there, but something had changed. I was struggling to put words around what I was feeling and sensing. Where once it was joy and wonder, now there was a foreboding that I was trying to grasp. What was I here to watch? What was I here to see?

I wasn't the only one to witness creation's sacrifice to clothe Adam and Eve. They saw it too. For the first time, I felt resentment toward them, and I wanted them punished for what they had done, not clothed. All of Eden seemed restless and fragile now, even the tree I was sitting in. Would it even hold me anymore? I've never thought of these thoughts before. Where were they coming from?

These animals had done nothing wrong. They hadn't eaten from the wrong *tree*! They hadn't even gone near it, and now their blood flowed into the ground. None of this was supposed to happen. None of it! I could feel anxiety soaring within me. I wanted to fly away and scream all at the same time. I wanted to find that strange lizard and tear it to shreds. But I didn't have the strength to soar, let alone fly. All I could do was weep.

As the tears fell, I became aware of an old friend sitting beside me again. Wisdom had returned, and this time she was crying with me. I needed Wisdom to be encouraging and tell me it was all part of the plan and that the love story was playing out just the way the Designer had meant it to. But Wisdom wept ...

After what seemed an age, Wisdom stirred and looked at me. The tears in her eyes were raw and shocking. It was as if I could see the pain of the wound that had been caused, and I had no idea how to fix it. Fix it? How can any of this be fixed? My friends are lying dead on the ground. I can smell the blood from where I am. I have no words ...

It was Wisdom that comforted me when Eve took the fruit. I felt I should have words to comfort her in this grief. But, no words would come.

Wisdom, without turning, opened her mouth and simply said, "Sometimes there are no words; there are only tears."

So, I sat for what seemed like an age and waited. I had been tasked with the job to watch and see, and that is what I would do. I had no words for Wisdom, but I was able to be present, and that is what I did. Eventually, Wisdom's tears ceased.

Still, I had no words, but I could sense that Wisdom was about to speak. So I waited, and I waited. When she finally spoke, her voice cracked, and the rawness of her grief had changed it. Again, she simply said, "Grief is something everyone needs to understand, Eagle, and it has the power to change your life."

Again, she went silent until she eventually said, "I know you have questions. Your grief will want to lash out and demand answers. It may also want to run and hide from all you have seen to pretend it didn't happen. When you are ready to ask them, first stop and let your talons feel the ground beneath you. Then, when you have soothed the anger, ask yourself, which *tree* in Eden are you sitting under?"

This question shocked me! "What do you mean?" I was so confused and could not understand what was happening in front of me, around me, and within me.

Wisdom simply nodded and said, "I know you are confused, and it's right that you are. You are watching Adam and Eve make choices that the Designer will not prevent. But, Eagle, do not let your confusion inspire a choice to eat fruit from the wrong *tree*."

I looked at her in shocked disbelief. I had, once again, lost my words.

Her soothing voice spoke again, "Are you asking your questions from *The Knowledge of Good and Bad* or from *The Tree of Life*?"

This confused me even more.

"But it was the Designer who sacrificed my friends! It wasn't Adam and Eve!" I said. "Wisdom! This is wrong!"

Wisdom nodded again and said, "Yes, that is true."

"But, it is wrong, Wisdom!"

"The Designer asked you to watch, Eagle. So far, all you have seen is your own grief and loss. Eagle, look at the Designer."

I looked and saw that His eyes were like Wisdom's. So raw was the pain I witnessed in Him.

"You feel the grief of such a great loss, Eagle. But know the grief you feel is also felt by Him. There was no joy in this for Him, and it grieved Him to do this."

I knew Wisdom was getting to a point, but it was beyond my grasp. Finally, my exasperation gave way to words spilling out from me, "He could have stopped all of this. He didn't need to feel this grief. I could have killed that strange lizard myself!"

"Yes," said Wisdom. "All of this was possible and could have been done had He taken part of their design away. He created them with the power of choice."

"But look what they did with their choice," I screamed back at Wisdom.

"Yes," Wisdom said gently, "Look what they did with their choice."

It was then that Wisdom turned back to me and said, "Remember the seed that needs to die? Do you remember when I told you this, and you didn't really understand? You must have thought of many other possible solutions."

Wisdom paused, but I knew there was more to come, and I wanted answers. Wisdom finally added, "So few have ever seen what you have seen ... so few ... which means you are seeing something entrusted to us, and the Designer trusts you and has designed you to see it."

Wisdom paused again before continuing, "Listen to me, Eagle. I am inviting you to understand something few others will understand. Many will question the Designer over this one event in the coming days, and He will be maligned, rejected, and scorned for this."

She paused, closed her eyes, and gathered her thoughts before saying, "But He will endure it, Eagle, and He will continue to let His actions reveal His heart. I invite you to see past all you have witnessed, the choices made, the death, the guilt, the shame, the strange lizard, and into the heart of what is unfolding in front of you. Yes, you feel grief, and it is right that you do. You feel the loss that Adam and Eve have brought to Eden, but more than that, you feel the grief of the Designer. Which also means you are also feeling the love of the Designer. Know this, Eagle, if there was no grief, there was no love."

Wisdom was right; I had never felt grief before, so I sat and felt it. Wisdom again leaned over and said, "Which *tree* are you sitting under Eagle?" It was then that I realized what Wisdom meant. If I sat under *The Tree of Knowledge of Good and Bad*, I would seek fault, judgment, and punishment. But to sit under *The Tree of Life* was to seek life in all of its fullness. The fullness of life is love. It has always been so, and now it is needed more than ever. To love is not to look for fault but for connection and restoration.

There are times when everything slows down in my life, and I have discovered these are times of great revelation. I turned again to the Designer, and I could see His love. I could see His desire for restoration and healing. I could see His hope that Adam and Eve would choose His love, but He would never force it upon them. For love to exist, choice needed to remain without control. Wisdom could easily see I was finally understanding, not by my words, but by my tears. There was no greater love than the love I witnessed right here in front of me. Their choices had brought consequences. Eden would close to them.

I realized I could have used my choice to destroy the strange lizard. But it was not my design to control others' choices, and the Designer trusted I would stay within His design for me. But in giving me choice, He also allowed me to break my design. He poured such love out on us all and would never control us. It is a gift, such a precious gift. I was free to do whatever I wanted, and with my freedom, I chose to eat from *The Tree of Life*. At this moment, I realized the magnitude of what the Designer had breathed into us all.

But there were still questions, and as I turned to Wisdom, I could see that familiar smile. There was sadness in the smile, as she knew I carried many unanswered questions. Before I could speak, she said, "You want to know why Adam and Eve needed to be clothed."

"Part of this answer is easy to understand. The other part, less so," Wisdom continued. "The easy part is this: Adam and Eve felt shame for the first time, and their response was to hide. They weren't looking for a few leaves to cover parts of their bodies. They were looking for all the leaves to cover all of their bodies." She continued, "It's what you would have done if you had killed the lizard."

Another slowing down moment was happening for me.

"You mean, if I killed the lizard, I would have been hiding with them?" I replied.

"Yes," said Wisdom. "Your anger was causing you to lose control and make decisions no longer aligned with your design. You would no longer be doing what the Designer had asked you to do, and death would have resulted."

This was more than I could comprehend. I had not realized how close I was to rejecting the Designer's words. At that moment, I looked up and saw the Designer's eyes on me. I felt such shame that I had let Him down. I had come so close to so quickly letting go of what He had given me to do. I had not understood ...

CHAPTER 4

"But what about the part that is less easy to understand?" I asked Wisdom.

Wisdom said, "You also want to know why your friends had to die. For that answer, you will have to ask the Designer."

This was my question, but I no longer wanted to ask it. I could not, I felt I had failed Him already, and I no longer felt worthy of being in His presence. So, I hid.

Would the Designer even want to look for me? Time passed, and when I opened my eyes, I saw that Wisdom was no longer sitting with me. In her place was the Designer. I nearly fell out of the tree. I stumbled over so many words I had wanted to say. Thousands of apologies formed in my mind, but none could communicate my feelings.

Then He spoke, "Eagle, do you love me?"

"Yes, Lord, I do love you," came falling from my mouth as tears rolled from my eyes.

"Eagle, watch over them," is what He said.

That familiar voice with healing in every word. The feeling of restoration made its way through every muscle, tendon, and feather. Whenever He spoke, I wanted to soar. It was everything within me to stay present. I was sitting next to the Designer, and I didn't want to miss a word.

He looked at me, smiled, and said, "I made you to soar, so soar! I will still be here when you get back. You have questions, and I want to answer them."

So, at His permission, I spread my wings and soared. Every word He had spoken only made me go higher and higher. It filled me with joy, hope, and love. Such love! It reminded me of when He created me. I didn't even know what flying was until He spoke the word "fly." His voice is creation, and when He said it, I knew that whatever flying was, I was about to do it. Now, I was back doing what His voice was speaking. I was soaring. I was feeling the wind move beneath my wings. Each gust was one of His breaths that allowed me to go higher. I'd never been this high before.

It was then that I realized what He wanted me to see. I could see far beyond Eden, beyond what even my powerful eyes could see. I could see His creation, and it was beautiful. Beaches, mountains, waterfalls, and forests. So extensive was His creation that I marveled at the wonder of it all. He hadn't just made Eden; He had made a world of wonder and discovery. As I looked closer, I could see the forests teaming with life. There was so much to discover and so much that I did not know. Then I heard His familiar voice calling me back to the tree.

As I landed and settled my feathers, I looked at Him in awe, and He looked back at me with such joy. He knew I had seen so much more of what He had created, and I had witnessed his goodness. This was a moment I will never forget. We were one, and there was no sense of disappointment within His gaze. I had expected something so different, but here He was, and His presence was changing me.

"You want to know why your friends had to die," He said.

"Yes, Lord, I do," I replied before continuing, "I don't understand."

"Few do," He responded. "And few will."

He paused before He continued, "You have been given the joy of seeing more. I know your sight can be both a blessing and a challenge on days like this. But I have not given you the commission to see what you want to see. I have commissioned you to see all that I show you. What you have known as Eden is simply my heart, no more and no less. But as you have now discovered, there is far more to see."

He paused before continuing, "All you have seen so far, even the death of two of your friends, is only a small part of what will unfold before you. Wisdom has shared small windows into the future. Some of these you will understand, and some will feel like a riddle you cannot solve. When she told you of the seed that needs to die, everything within you wanted that riddle solved, and one day it will be, but today is not that day. There is so much more, but in time all things will become clear."

Then he continued, "But first, let me share with you about your friends. To do that, I have first to help you understand shame."

"Sit back, Eagle; this could take a while," he said. "Just remember, you see my heart laid bare, every part of it. I have withheld nothing from you. But to see it in fullness and truth, we must sit beneath *The Tree of Life*. Many will look upon my heart from a distance, always wondering if they can come close. Many will enter, but they will use their choice to judge me rather than dine with me."

"Eagle, do you love me?" He said again.

"Yes, Lord, with everything I am, I love you," I replied.

"Come and dine with me under *The Tree of Life*," He replied.

I flew to the ground and let my feathers all find their place as I walked across the ground to him. Walking has always been odd to me. I do it for very short distances, but it is not my preferred way. But I didn't care how it looked; I wanted to be with Him. With all that had happened on this day, He had time for me.

He opened His hands and offered me a portion of food I had never seen before. It looked like bread, but it wasn't. When I looked at Him, He smiled and said, "This is the bread of my Kingdom. In the years ahead, it will be called 'manna'."

I took it and ate it. It had the texture of bread, but the taste was sweet. Something about it calmed my spirit and settled me beside Him.

"Eagle, let your talons go down into the ground." I did as He asked me. I had never done this before, but as I did, He continued, "What do you feel?"

"Lord, I feel life ... and ... I feel death. The blood of my friends is here in the ground," I said, shocked.

"Yes," He said. "Now, what else do you feel?"

"I feel sorrow ... I feel disappointment ... I feel loneliness ... But there is something deeper than all of that ..." I said.

"Yes, Eagle. What is it?" He asked.

"Lord, I feel LOVE! Such deep, deep love. I can't touch this for too long. My Lord! It is overwhelming me."

"Eagle, don't let go. Allow yourself to feel this love. What is it doing to you?" He said.

Even though this love overwhelmed me, I believed Him when He said I could hold on. I felt the love flowing up my talons, into my legs, then into my body, like it was seeking something within me. But what?

"Eagle, can you find the fear within you? The fear that drove you to hide up there in the tree?" He asked.

"Lord, I cannot feel it. Where did it go?"

"Eagle, remember, you are feeling my heart. I am holding nothing back from you. When you drove your talons into the ground, you felt the sorrow and disappointment of shame, and you also felt the loneliness of shame. But that is not the only thing I wanted you to feel. I wanted you to feel the healing of shame. I wanted you to feel joy. I wanted you to feel my approval. I wanted you to feel our connection."

He continued, "Most will not hold the ground as you have held it. Some will think I am an angry Lord and look for my punishment. They will claim to see my judgment when the earth shakes or when the thunder roars. All that means is they let go before discovering the depth of my love. Then, some will think I'm a distant Lord, never coming close and never interacting with them. This will result from people hiding from me and choosing not to come close."

"Many of these people will create what they call 'theologies' about me. They will write and teach about me but never know me. They will assume my character and my words but never listen to a word I have spoken to them. This will happen when they hide and avoid my love; the darkness they surround themselves with will become a breeding ground for knowledge about me, but not the understanding of me."

He paused, but this time He smiled as He spoke, "Some, though, will come with their questions, as you did. They will find what they seek and discover the power of my love. They will testify to their healing even as you have just experienced it. But they will also find much more than that; they will discover my heart."

He paused before pointing, "Can you see Adam and Eve over there? They are yet to encounter the fullness of the love you have felt, and I long for them to be healed as you have been today."

"I long for them to sit under this *tree* with me and receive the goodness I had long ago prepared for them to live in. My design is that they would heal in this place and not fear it. I will do anything for them because I love them. There is no sacrifice I would not make for them. And today, they chose not to sit with me under *the Tree of Knowledge of Good and Bad*. They decided the feelings of sorrow, disappointment, and even loneliness were more than they could take. So, I clothed them with a precious and invaluable gift. With this gift, I had hoped they would at least see my love for them. Eagle, I am sorry that your friends died; it's a grief that I also share."

The Designer was silent for a time before He spoke again, "You are here, though, to see more than you are watching. Do you want to see more?"

"Yes, my Lord, I want to see. I want to understand."

"Place your talons in the ground again," He said.

I closed my eyes and allowed my talons to slip beneath the surface.

"Can you still feel death?" He said.

His question shocked me. I wasn't expecting the Designer to ask me this, and I felt sure I would feel the blood of my friends still held within the ground. My talons reached deep beyond the sorrow, disappointment, and loneliness, and they even now felt strangely at home in the love. But I could not feel the death of my friends. So I pressed deeper and deeper, sure that I would eventually find death, but I could not. I was so lost in what I was doing that I didn't hear the Designer laughing at first. I was so confused by this.

I responded, "Lord, I can not find the blood of my friends."

The Designer allowed His smile to erupt into laughter, "The one who occupied the strange lizard believes that death has a power greater than mine."

I have never heard the Designer laugh like this. Everything in Eden came alive at the sound of His joy. Even Adam and Eve turned to stare at him, looking as confused as I must have. I could feel His joy, and at the same time, I could also feel the grief deep inside of Him.

Once He stopped, He said, "Death is never the end. I have the final voice. Never doubt this, or forget this, Eagle." He said before continuing, "Oh, people will still make their theologies of death, strange lizards, and something that they will eventually call 'sin'. But all of these are dust under my feet. I am the source of life. Through me, all things exist and have life. Your friends, Eagle, are alive in me."

He went silent for a moment before He continued, "These theologies, strange lizards, and sins will melt like wax before me. Do not be fooled by people who claim to know me but have never sat here with me. You have, Eagle, and you have felt my love. To feel my love is to know me. Knowing me manifests love and life, not death."

"My Lord, there are things you speak of that are beyond what I can understand or comprehend. I do not know what 'theologies' even are."

"They will be people's best guess at my character."

"Why would they guess at your character when they can know it simply by spending time with you?" I asked.

"That is the question not even I can answer, Eagle."

The Designer went silent for a time before He looked back at the ground that still held the stain of my animal friend's life source.

Then He continued, "For now, Adam and Eve have chosen their path, and I have clothed them with the costliest garment I could. I love them too much to let them feel they always need to hide from me. For now, the clothes will make do. But eventually, from the seed Wisdom told you about, One will come who will make this much clearer to them, to you, and to all of my creation. He will invite them to sit at the *Tree of Life* again."

"When or how will this all happen?" I asked.

The Designer bowed his head and smiled as He often did. After a few moments, He lifted His head and, with the same smile, said, "Soon, Eagle, it will be soon." Then He continued, "With that being said, I want to show you one more thing in the ground if you are willing to see it."

"I am, my Lord."

"You are courageous, Eagle, and you agree to do things even before you understand what I'm offering you."

"If it is something of your creation, my Lord, I want to see it."

"Place your talons back into the ground. Go through all of the feelings you have encountered before. See, the more you place your talons into the ground, the greater the healing you experience. You are at one with me, and I am at one with you."

I let my talons sink into the ground again, as He asked.

"Yes, my Lord, again, I can feel your love. And again, my Lord, I can feel it is overwhelming me."

"You will notice you are able to hold it for longer. Each time you feel my love, you will understand my love greater."

I sat with my talons in the ground for so long that time disappeared. Not knowing if I was there for a moment, an hour, or for days. I did not want to leave, as all I could feel was His love pulsing through every part of my body. My animal friends were alive again. My love for Adam and Eve grew, and my disappointment melted away. Everything within me wanted to fly to them and be with them.

"Eagle, there is more I want to show you."

His voice broke me out of the vision. I looked down and saw my talons were now deep into the soft earth.

"Eagle, go deeper."

At that, I closed my eyes and sunk my talons deeper than they had been before. At the extent of the love, I felt something familiar but also different.

Then I realized what I was feeling. "My Lord, I feel blood again," I exclaimed. "Whose blood is this? I know of no other animal that has died."

He reached over and placed His hand on me, and as He touched me, I was shocked by a vision.

"My Lord, the blood ... it's yours."

I released my talons from the ground and all but collapsed into His arms.

"My Lord, I do not understand. Why is your blood in the ground?" I exclaimed.

"You won't understand it now, but you will in the days ahead. Life flows through the blood, and you have seen how death has tried to stop it, but in My love is the life I have so freely poured into all things. That is what you felt."

There was silence for a time before the Designer spoke to me again, "Eagle, the blood was not the only thing you saw, was it?"

"No, my Lord, but I do not understand what I saw."

"What did you see?"

"My Lord, I saw a scene flash in front of my eyes for only the shortest of moments. I saw a dead tree."

There was another long silence before the Designer got up to leave. As He did, he smiled and said, "You have seen true, my friend."

CHAPTER 5

Amongst the shock I had just experienced, another question came tumbling out of my mouth, "Wait. My Lord," I yelled. "Why does Eden need to close?"

"Eagle, for that answer, you are going to have to come on a journey with me," the Designer smiled as He said this. "And remember, I said it was for a time, not forever."

I watched as the Designer went back to Adam and Eve. The love He had for them was tangible. Even now, nothing was being withheld from them, but what they clung to the most were the new clothes He had made for them. I could hear Him speaking to them about the challenges that were ahead outside of Eden.

This was another slowing down moment for me … "outside of Eden"… outside of the Designer's heart … It began making sense to me; shame could not remain in the Designer's heart. Even now, would the Designer have let them stay in Eden if they had chosen to reach deeper, past the sorrow, disappointment, and separation they were feeling? But He wouldn't make them do anything they wouldn't choose. After everything I had just experienced, I wanted to rush to them and tell them of a more profound and powerful love than all the pain and shame they were feeling.

Then Wisdom appeared next to me, and I already knew the words I was about to hear. "Eagle, they have often walked with Him in the cool of the evening. They know His love, and they know where to find it. They have let go of His words."

Wisdom paused before continuing, "It won't always be like this. As you have heard the Designer say, they will come to understand this love, and one day you will see them again sitting under *The Tree of Life*."

I sat with Wisdom for hours, thinking of everything I had witnessed. The Designer was right; some of it I wished I had never seen. But, then again, if I had not seen it, I would never be able to understand what I felt. And that dead tree ... I didn't know what to make of it.

The sun was setting, and as usual, everything in Eden stopped to watch it happen. This painful day was at its end. We sat and watched the colors of the sky slowly change. Darkness would soon settle over Eden, and Adam and Eve would be gone by the time when it lifted.

That evening, angels came into Eden. I had seen them before, but this time they looked different. Gone was the carefree attitude and the willingness to engage and enjoy the Designer's magnificent creation. This time they came with flaming swords and stood resolute, preventing access to *The Tree of Life*. Nothing would pass by them, and Eden was closed for a time. The *two trees* would continue to grow and thrive in the middle of Eden, but now Adam and Eve could not look upon them. Nor will they be able to put their fingers into the soil beneath the *Tree of Life*.

That night, I sat high in a tree and pondered everything I had witnessed. So much had changed in such a brief space of time. I was remembering brilliant times when I would watch the Designer walk and play with Adam and Eve. Their laughter would fill Eden, and their joy affected every part of His creation. Nothing was withheld from them, and everything thrived with life and abundance. But I will never forget that strange lizard and the words that it spoke ... those words needed to be remembered for when that strange lizard, or whatever form it took next, would dare to speak again.

But what I will remember most is the grief of those moments when shame flowed from a voice, and then it became a choice. I would soon learn that once it became a choice, their identity would be next to change. That could be one of the hardest things to heal.

If shame had seeded itself in my life and I had killed that lizard, my identity would have changed. Maybe I would have been known as the bringer of death. Maybe all my friends would have feared me and what I could do to them. Maybe I, too, would beg for somewhere to hide from the shame that filled me.

But, I had touched healing and discovered so much more. My talons reached deep into the ground, giving me the healing my spirit craved. 'From the ground, this healing would come' ... slowly, Wisdom's words were coming back to me, and they were making sense ... what was it she said? "The seed had to go into the ground and die before new life would come." It was something like that. So what is the seed? Where will it come from? What fruit will grow from that seed? Did that dead tree have anything to do with the seed that had to die? I could feel the truth of Wisdom's words, but to picture it eluded me.

While deep in thought, I hadn't even noticed the sunrise, and I definitely didn't notice the Designer sitting beside me. The shock of it all snapped me out of my thoughts and back into the present. The Designer whistled a tune I had heard before but had trouble placing until He spoke. He looked over everything He had created and said, "It is good." Then I realized, He always whistled when He was resting and gazing over all He had created.

He was just waiting for me. The next chapter of this great love story was about to unfold, and He wanted me to see it, and he wanted me to understand it.

"Eagle," He said, "From this day forward, I'm inviting you to record everything you see. As I said, some things will be great and mighty, while others will break your heart. Remember, at any time, you can reach deeply into the ground and touch the love that flows through all things and holds all things together. Never forget this love, and know that it is always there. Even in your worst moments, when you have made your greatest mistakes, it is still there, and nothing can separate you from my love, nothing."

Once He finished speaking, he simply said, "Come Eagle, I want you to meet two brothers. Their names are Cain and Abel."

CHAPTER 6

But before we get to the brothers, yes, there were two of them, and they could not be more different. Cain came first, and not long after, Abel was born. Cain was curious about everything. To him, every problem needed a solution. Abel, though, was a lad who enjoyed being with the animals. He was easy to be around, and love flowed easily from him. I had seen and followed them many times before, but my charge was first to watch Adam and Eve. It was them I knew best. But to understand the brothers, you must start with the parents.

Adam and Eve did not just leave with the new clothing the Designer had given them. They left with their two young boys, boys who had raced through Eden. I could never keep up with them. They would run, hide, swim, climb, and wrestle everywhere they could find. *The Tree of Knowledge of Good and Bad* was the only thing off-limits to them. Adam had constantly reminded them of the dangers of that *tree*. Many times I had watched cautiously as they pointed it out and talked about it, but they never went close to it. These two brothers often walked with their parents in the cool of the evening when the Designer walked with them. They knew His voice, and they loved His presence.

They both felt the impact of that fateful day when Adam and Eve ate from that tree. It had been one of those ordinary days when they were running through Eden and having the times of their lives. They'd even found a new swimming hole. Eden was shining in all of its created splendor that day. The place they discovered was so beautiful they felt they needed to share it with their parents.

Their excitement had them competing to see who could tell their parents first. The usual playful wrestle became a fight somewhere between the swimming hole and the *Tree of Knowledge of Good and Bad*. Neither of them had encountered these feelings before, but something had changed in Eden. The race had become a battle that needed to be won. It was no longer about the discovery of the swimming hole. It was now about being the one to win.

By the time they had gotten to the *two trees*, they could not find their parents. They were gone, so they called and called to them. They looked for them everywhere they could think of, but Eden was silent. As they stopped, they looked at each other and realized they were bleeding because of the fighting. Something wasn't right, and they both could feel it. The atmosphere had changed, and they had never felt like this toward each other before.

Then, the strange lizard crawled out from the bushes and said, "Your parents are in there," pointing to where he came from. As he pointed, a hideous laugh came out of him. Before the brothers could go and find their parents, he said, "Look on the ground. What do you see? What tree do you think that fruit came from?" Then another hideous laugh dripped out of him.

Lying on the ground was a piece of fruit with two bites taken from it. The brothers looked at each other and instantly knew what had happened. Neither had eaten the fruit; it could only have been their parents.

Everything in Eden was still unsettled, and I could feel it in the tree I was sitting in, and now I could sense it within the hearts of the two brothers.

What they experienced next happened quickly. Their parents emerged from the bushes but were covered in leaves they had somehow tied together. They'd never seen them like this, and none of it made sense. Before they could ask, "why?" they heard the Designer walking through Eden. However, instead of walking straight to them, He called their parents. It was like He didn't know where they were. The confusion for the brothers was now overwhelming. The fight they had was now a memory. In their minds was a series of events happening outside of their control. They were caught up in their parent's actions, and their situation was changing through no fault of their own. They were so young and innocent, and their parents were lost in their shame.

I watched as the Designer made His way through Eden, but this is a story I have told before. Why didn't Adam and Eve respond to His voice with the love it carried? How strong was this thing that would become known as shame? Could they not see it had already affected their sons?

At that moment, Wisdom flew up beside me and said, "Eagle, shame is a disease, and if left untreated, it will affect all the people surrounding them and flow to the generations that follow them. Its sole purpose is to corrupt the design of their life, and it will lay siege to how they love the Designer, those around them, and themselves. These two brothers will grow to experience this, but we will see if they really ever understand it?"

Then she continued, "Eagle, I have spoken to you about a seed that needs to go into the ground and die before life comes. Shame is another seed that will produce another kind of fruit; it is not a fruit to eat."

"Many people will condemn the Designer, believing His stance condemned Adam and Eve. But those who will say such things were not there to witness these moments. They will form so-called 'theologies' that condemn the very ones the Designer created in His image and loved with every fiber of His being. No, the Designer did not condemn them, and He loved them and would never take their choice from them and control them. What you are witnessing is a love that goes beyond reason. But, Eagle, when has reason ever been the foundation stone of love?"

Wisdom was quiet for a while, but I could see she was still thinking, and then she started to smile.

"Wisdom, why are you smiling?" I asked.

"Love will never fully fit into a plan, a teaching, or a structure. It operates beyond reason, beyond knowledge, and even beyond understanding. Eagle, you will do the craziest things because of love."

She continued, "People will even say the Designer's character changed over time and that the Designer of Eden was not the same as one of the later stories. These so-called 'theologies' will come from ones who cannot see what we have seen nor experience what we have felt. They will not know the love that operates beyond their reason and will not see that He loves everyone uniquely. Many, many years from this time, a writer in His story will say of Him, 'He is the same yesterday, today, and forever.' That writer, like us, will have seen and known Him."

I sat and thought through all Wisdom was saying. These future events were beyond my comprehension, but His love was not.

"Have you not known His great love through all the years we have been with Him?" She asked.

I replied, "No wisdom; there has not been a time where I did not know His love. It makes me shudder to even wonder what it would be like without it. I have never had cause to question His love, but now I feel that I will have even more questions about His love."

That fateful day when Eden closed, the Designer's and Wisdom's words kept ringing in my ears "the seed needed to die … it needed to be sown into the ground for it to live again." Was this always the planned design?

I stayed in my tree, watching and listening to everything happening. It was everything that I could do to hold myself in place and not try to escape those moments. Hearing my Lord close off access by Adam and Eve to *The Tree of Life* was too much grief for me to bear. No one had lost access to that *tree* before, and all of us had tasted and seen the goodness that it held. However, now, Eden stood silent.

The silence had gone on so long that it felt like He was waiting for Adam and Eve to cry out for release from bondage. Until this day, they were able to look Him in the eye and celebrate every moment of every day with Him. Today, though, this seemed like a distant memory. So great was their sorrow that every animal in Eden released their own voices for them. The sound of Eden erupted all around me, but Adam and Eve were still silent.

When the Designer spoke, He simply asked, "Where were you?"

Adam finally spoke, "I heard you walking, my Lord, and I was afraid. I have never felt these feelings before. I was naked, and I feared you seeing me this way."

The Designer took a deep breath, and even though He knew the answer, He still asked, "Did you eat from the *tree* I told you not to?"

At that very moment, I closed my eyes and remembered putting my talons into the ground and feeling the sorrow, the disappointment, and the loneliness. I felt the pain of my mistake. That pain was so real that I wanted to release myself from it. I would have if I were not invited to go deeper through the pain to find the depth of His love. I don't know how long I was lost in the power of His love, but in my mind's eye, I saw the Designer sitting under *The Tree of Life*, inviting Adam and Eve to do the same. My soul rejoiced at seeing this, and it felt so real. They were feeling the healing power of the Designer. It was another moment in which I wanted to soar again. But, it was then that I became aware of Wisdom's wing on me. I was so excited to tell her what I had seen, but I only saw tears when I looked at her, I only saw tears. I turned back to the Designer, and they weren't under *The Tree of Life*; they were walking out of Eden.

"No!" I screamed. "This can not be."

"Yes," Wisdom whispered. "This is the way it will be, but not forever. Adam and Eve chose this path, and they will walk it. But it will not be easy for them. They will now have to work the ground to produce their food. Relationships will also become harder for them as they learn to live with their shame rather than let the Designer heal it."

"No," came from my mouth again, but this time it was not a scream … it was a whisper.

Wisdom drew me in and said, "Watch this."

I watched as the family walked from Eden, but what I saw restored hope into my spirit. The family was leaving, and I noticed that strange lizard as they did. But this time, I would not let it get near this family. It had done enough destruction this day, and I would lay down my own life so that this family could be saved.

"No!" Wisdom spoke directly and powerfully to me. "You were told to watch, and you will need to see this."

I looked again, and the strange lizard was no longer crawling. Where did its legs go? It was now slithering straight to Eve. As it opened its mouth, I felt like I was watching a bad dream all over again. My mind was racing, "No, Eve. Don't listen to the lizard." But then the most unexpected thing happened. Eve trod on the lizard's head and crushed it under her heel. It didn't even get to utter a word. It lay motionless under her foot. The lizard had died. My thoughts raced back to hearing the Designer say to Adam about the forbidden *tree*, "This fruit was not to be eaten, or death would result." The strange lizard had eaten its fill, and now it was dead.

What I saw next gave me even more hope. The Designer did not stay in Eden. He followed them, walking with them every step of the way. They could feel His presence, and somehow I knew His love would break into their hearts again, healing all the pain that prevented them from releasing their shame.

Now I could fly. I would follow the Designer and watch over the ones He had commissioned me to watch.

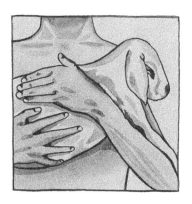

CHAPTER 7

This is my favorite time of day, the morning. The day is new, and everything about it is fresh. I love to feel the sun on my feathers; it reminds me of the day I was created. The mistakes of yesterday are now in the past, and the hopes of today are in front of me. So, I take off, and I soar. My task is to watch and listen, which is what I plan to do.

As I take flight, I can already see Cain and Abel out in the fields. Cain is tending the soil, and his crop fields go on and on. I can see wheat, corn, barley, and ones I have yet to learn the names of. Cain knows them all, though, and he tends to them well. Abel is on the other side of the valley, and I can see him leading flocks of sheep to greener grass. He seems to know where to lead them to find the best food.

The beauty of the Designer's work is laid out in every direction. There are snow-capped mountains and beautiful valleys. Some forests seemed to go on forever, and I have explored them as far as my wings would take me. I marvel at the Designer's work in every direction. It's not just the things I see; it's the things I feel that speak to me of His design. On the ground, I feel warmth permeating every part of my body. When I'm soaring higher, it's the coolness of the air I feel throughout my body. I still do not understand everything, but I love every part of His design and want to experience it all.

At first, I was stunned to see so many animals outside of Eden. I thought Eden held most of them. How wrong I was. I even met many more eagles. Each of them was tasked as I was, and each was protective of the ones the Designer had entrusted to them.

Many have called Eden "Paradise," and it truly is. However, I see many trees out here like I perched in and soared above in Eden: the same flowers, plants, fruits, and vegetables. Everything I see is something that the Designer declared "good."

Much time has passed since they left Eden, and now more and more people are making their homes all over the lands beyond my eyesight. The Designer had told them to be fruitful and multiply, which is what they had done. His design was clearly working outside of Eden.

Cain is an incredible farmer here, and his crops feed many. He has learned to work the hard ground. In the early days, the harvests were sparse, but Cain has mastered his craft, and I marvel at his ingenuity. It was Cain who first wondered about bending the great river called The Euphrates, a river flowing with such power and life-giving water. He stood for hours by its banks, asking the river to give up its water to irrigate the fields. At first, people laughed at him and called him foolish. But it wasn't long before they saw nothing would get in his way. He found it wasn't hard to dig new channels for water to flow through to the fields. Then the river gave up its water, and the land benefited from its abundance and Cain's ingenuity. He seemed to master everything he put his hand to. There was no problem that he could not fix, but he was also a man who liked to work alone.

It was a joy to watch him at work, and he didn't seem to mind me watching all he was doing. He was so proud of his work, and as each harvest grew, his reputation grew. Somehow, the Designer telling his parents that the ground would be hard to work made him work harder to show he could do it. He is a problem solver, to that, there is no doubt.

Abel, though, was different. At first, it was hard for me to see it because the two brothers loved to spend all their time together. But after many years, I could see the differences between the two boys. Abel was so willing to love people well. He was like Cain, and he succeeded where others had not. However, he didn't follow Cain to become a farmer but a shepherd. Such different paths, and as they each immersed themselves in their own, they spent less and less time together. It was then I could start to see their different personalities.

As I soar over Abel's flocks today, I can see hundreds, if not thousands, of sheep below me. From this height, they look like little clouds on the ground, and each of them is so white and soft to the touch. These sheep know Abel's voice. They only have to hear his whistle, and they quickly respond to their master. He always seems to know where they are and where they need to feed next.

It was Abel that discovered that a sheep could be shorn. Their wool grew fast and did not fall out like my feathers or other animal's coats. The burden of their wool soon became obvious to Abel, so he fashioned a flint into what he called a "knife" and could cut the fleece without hurting the sheep. Abel's wife, Miriam, discovered the fleece could be made into a yarn that could be knitted to make clothes. Not one sheep had to die for the people to be clothed.

Abel loved working with people; today, as I soar, I can see all the people helping him. He's taken many under his wing, and they have learned all that Abel has discovered. He takes great joy in being able to pass on all he has learned.

One day, I overheard Abel's conversation with one of his apprentices. The apprentice asked, "Where did you learn all of this from?"

Abel's smile was enormous; he loved discussing how he had discovered these things.

He replied, "The Designer, of course. He taught me everything I know. He taught me about the sheep's wool; the best grasses for them to eat; how to care for each of them; and especially, how to love them. I owe everything to Him."

Abel then fell silent for a moment and pondered all he had learned.

After a while, the apprentice asked him another question, "Abel, you were in Eden. Please, tell me again what you felt there."

Abel had been asked this question many times before, and tears would rise in his eyes each time he responded, "I felt love. I felt love in its most pure form. Knowing this love is to know that there is nothing you cannot do. It is life, and it's in everything. There, I felt connected to all things and lived without shame. I lived free from fear."

What I loved about Abel was he continued to love as he had been loved in Eden. He knew love could be reproduced, and it never lessened in him. He also knew that shame could be healed. In the days after they left Eden, I had watched Abel, day after day, sit with the Designer. There were some days he sat and hardly moved with his hands resting on the ground. These moments in His presence were so powerful, and the Designer loved them too.

One of the days, as I sat in my tree, I noticed Wisdom sitting beside me. I always loved it when Wisdom would do this. Something about her presence and voice brought me so much peace. I remember the early days of her calming my soul with her words. She always seemed to know when to turn up.

I turned to Wisdom and asked, "What is the Designer saying to Abel?"

She replied, "Do you remember when the Designer invited you to sit under *The Tree of Life* with Him?"

"Yes," I replied, "How could I ever forget it?"

"This is what the Designer is doing with Abel. He is learning what has been placed deep within the ground, and the Designer is revealing His love to Him."

"But Eden is closed. How could Abel feel what I felt?" I replied.

"His love and presence are not bound by a location, Eagle. Wherever He is, there is love," she said, continuing, "Abel is learning this right now. Look to see how his hands and feet go into the ground. He is discovering healing beyond the sorrow, beyond the disappointment, and beyond the loneliness. The Designer is now inviting him to press through the pain so that he can experience the healing of His love."

I pondered this for a long time. Then suddenly, the revelation hit me, and I blurted out to Wisdom, "He is love. I have always known this, Wisdom, and I have said it before. But the more I see it, the more I want to declare it."

She simply smiled and said, "Eagle, you are blessed by this knowledge. He is indeed love. What you are now feeling is your knowledge becoming a deeper understanding. You've known it all along and felt it at *The Tree of Life*. What has been added today is that it does not matter where you love Him. Eden may be closed, but the Designer's heart will never be closed to those who choose to love Him."

I knew at that moment there was still much more for me to know about the Designer and His love.

The same question I had long ago asked the Designer came tumbling out of my mouth, "Why, then, is Eden closed at all? Why not just let those who love Him come back into Eden and eat from *The Tree of Life*?"

Wisdom sat back, but this time with a sad smile, she said, "You have heard the Designer's answer to your question before. This will happen, Eagle, but not yet. Remember, the seed must go back into the ground and die. When you see this happen, you will know that Eden has been opened up once again."

It was the same riddle that Wisdom and the Designer had shared with me, and it continued to confound me. I don't fully understand it yet, but I believe I will. It is becoming clearer, and I believe it is connected to *The Tree of Life*. But why do they only speak of one seed? Are there not many seeds in every fruit of every tree? What was peculiar about this seed was that there was only one. Would there only be one other *Tree of Life*? And what was that dead tree?

I remember a particular day with Abel and the Designer so well. By the time Abel got up from the ground, the cool evening had turned into the dark of night. The Designer was no longer sitting with him, but the most peculiar thing had happened: Abel glowed. Light was flowing from deep within him. I could not tell if Abel knew he was glowing, but every step he made was illuminated by the light flowing from him. I could feel Abel's joy. It was like we were bound by that joy. It was a feeling of healing, of restoration, and yes, it was the love I felt in Eden. That night, I soared into the sky. Simply encountering His love always made me want to fly higher and higher and then hurtle to the ground and do it all again. These were days when I began to understand that love and freedom could not be separated. When I encountered that love, I felt free.

Eagles don't usually fly at night, but that particular night I did. I flew and screeched out to all creation of the wonders I had just witnessed. I could see animals and people waking up as I did, but I did not care. They needed to see what I was witnessing. Through sleepy eyes, they watched a man walk in the light of the Designer's love. Such a sight had not been seen since Eden.

CHAPTER 8

I had watched my charges for many years when one day, I noticed a new apprentice with Abel preparing a gift for the Designer. The apprentice was young, and his questions were many. Pointing to the lamb in Abel's arms, he said, "Abel, why are you taking this gift?"

It wasn't the first time he was asked this, and every time he would respond in the same way, "I freely give to Him because the Designer freely gave to me."

The apprentice loved his answer, but I saw another question burning within him. "Abel, why are you giving the very best of your flock to the Designer?"

Abel smiled at this, saying, "Because He has given me the best." Then, turning to his flock and the surrounding fields, he continued, "All that I have learned, I have discovered in His presence. He has held nothing back from me, and I love Him with everything I have. So today, this is the lamb I will take to Him."

I could see there were other questions brewing in the apprentice. He wondered how much more he could get at the market for this beautiful lamb. But Abel would not hear it. He gave freely to everyone, and today he gave his very best to the one who loved him powerfully.

On this day, both brothers would bring a gift for the Designer. I knew what Abel's was, but I did not know what Cain's would be. So I took flight to find him. When I did, I was surprised that there was no gift prepared. Cain had such an abundance he could give from. His harvests were plentiful, with so much wheat, corn, and fruit from his trees. Surely he had it prepared somewhere, and I had not found it yet. So I searched. When I could not find it, I returned to his barn and sat in a tree. I waited to see the magnitude and wonder of Cain's gift.

Again, I became aware of Wisdom beside me. I could never understand how she could do this without making a noise. As I turned, I could see she did not appear hopeful of finding Cain's gift. I could feel something else flowing through her.

"Wisdom, what are you feeling?" I asked.

She was quiet for a long time. Then before she found her words, she would quickly open and then close her mouth. Like words were there to come out, but she was unsure if she wanted to speak them.

Finally, she said, "Eagle, do you remember this time last year when we both sat here and waited for the gift to be presented?"

"Yes," I said. "It was not at all what I expected, and I remember it was not the best to come from the ground that Cain had worked."

"What about the year before that?" she said before letting me answer, "Or the year before that?"

I began to realize what Wisdom was saying was true. I knew she was waiting for the conclusion to form in my mind; she liked me discovering my own answers.

"Cain is not giving the best of his harvest," I said as the words trailed off my tongue.

But then my mind started putting together all the events I had witnessed over that time, and somewhere in there, I started comparing Cain's gifts to Abel's. Abel's gifts were far superior.

Wisdom snapped me out of it by answering my thoughts. "Eagle, comparison will always lead us to sit under the wrong *tree*. Do not think of this as others might. Think of it as if you were sitting under *The Tree of Life*. What do you hear when you sit under that *tree*?"

I closed my eyes to think, remember, and clear my mind of the comparisons I was making. My mind had already determined that Abel was better than Cain. These were the thoughts that Wisdom wanted me to capture and bring to *The Tree of Life*. As I started again, my mind soared back through the past and reclaimed the things I had seen. I remembered the two brothers fighting that day when Eve took the first bite of the fruit of *The Tree of Knowledge of Good and Bad*. I remembered Cain being so distraught at having to leave Eden. His little mind could not comprehend all that was happening, and I clearly remember him walking alone from Eden. Even then, I wondered why Adam and Eve had not come alongside him and comforted him. He was alone ...

I could remember many times when Abel would sit with the Designer in the cool of the evening. But with Cain, I could only recall a few times, and at no time did he walk away with the same glow within him that I saw in Abel. In fact, I remember him playing in the dirt like he was bored. It did not matter how often he was invited to dig deeper into the ground to feel the love. He only wanted to dig deeper into the ground he had tilled. He only wanted to prove that it was not as hard as the Designer had told them and that his produce was a testimony to his effort.

I then realized I was feeling what Wisdom was feeling. She felt the pain of one who did not want to be healed. Cain did not want to be healed; he only wanted to be right.

"But Wisdom, I have seen the Designer go to Cain as many times as he went to Abel. How is it that one brother is so different from the other?"

"Eagle, you will see this many times in the years to come, many times. The Designer will always work from and with His design and never deviate from it. Long ago, I told you this was the beginning of the greatest love story ever. You are witnessing that love story play out in joy and grief, freedom and sorrow, and connection and rejection. There is always a choice; never forget that. You are watching their choices play out right in front of you today."

Cain's powerful voice again broke up my thoughts. He was yelling at someone, and it took me a moment to understand what he was saying. He seemed frustrated, even angry, with the person he was addressing.

"Go to the barn and get something for the Designer. Don't take it from the front; that is for my family and me. Take it from the back," he barked.

A quiet response came from his apprentice, and it sounded like he was fearful. "Sir, the grain from the back has mildew in it, and the rats have been at it."

Cain roared back at him, "Find some that doesn't have mildew on it then and doesn't look like the rats have been at it."

At that, Cain stormed off. The apprentice was left unsure of what to do. Everyone knew of the way Abel would bring his finest gift. Everyone knew of the Designer's love for the time Abel spent with him. He knew disobeying Cain was not right, but he also knew what Cain told him to do was wrong.

Then, the apprentice seemed to be remembering words Abel had once spoken to him. He began whispering to himself, "Which *tree* are you sitting under? *The Tree of Knowledge of Good and Bad,* or *the Tree of life.* One will always lead you to think about right and wrong, and the other will think about life and love. Let this guide your thoughts."

At that, the apprentice got up, went straight to the grain he was told not to select from, and took the very best of it. He arranged it in the wagon to make it look like he had obeyed but knew he was bringing Cain's best to the sacrifice.

Wisdom and I sat and waited for Cain to go to the Designer's gift-giving time. When he did, he cast an eye over the cart, grunted, and got on, saying under his breath, "Let's get this over with. We all know whose gift is going to be preferred anyway."

The gift-giving time had come, so Wisdom and I flew off together. I always love it when we fly together. Something about her presence always inspires me to go higher and faster. She's always stretching me and inviting me to see more. She loves to show me things I do not know and take me places I have not been. This time, though, it felt different. Everything we had just witnessed with Cain had left an uneasy feeling. Everyone called this a celebration and feast time, but for me, the joy I longed for had been stolen.

This was traditionally a time when families gathered. Wisdom and I could see them coming from miles around. Each of them was carrying food for the feast. Seeing an entire family moving as one and coming together to celebrate was truly glorious. We could hear the joy in their voices. There was excessive energy in the children as they wondered who would be there, and whether they would be allowed to run off and play. There was always such a sense of excitement. It was a time I truly loved. The Designer would meet with them all, and I knew He also loved every moment of it.

Wisdom flew beside me, pointed down at Cain's cart, and said, "Look closely Eagle. Can you see what is coiled up beside Cain?"

What appeared to be a coiled rope or whip was alive. I did not need to ask what it was, as I instantly knew.

Wisdom said, "Remember, Eagle, you can watch, but you must know that this is Cain's moment. He must be the one to recognize the voice talking to him, and he must be the one who crushes it under his foot."

So many memories came rushing back to me. My mind hurtled back to when I was sitting in a tree with Wisdom watching a similar series of events unfold. I could clearly see and hear what was happening all over again. Cain's ears were open to the snake, and its forked tongue was weaving a tale of favoritism and exclusion.

It hissed, "You have worked this cursed ground, not Abel. It was you. You deserve to be honored for all your hard work. Think about all the sacrifices you have made to please the Designer and the disappointment at not being recognized."

I had been so focused on the hissing that I hadn't realized Wisdom was gone. When I looked, I could see her soaring over Abel. I flew straight to her; she didn't even mention Cain to me or say anything about the talking snake. She pointed me to a similar coil near Abel, but it was on the ground and was not moving. It would have looked like a rope lying on the ground to anyone else, but I could see it was not. The snake was dead, and Abel's footprint was on its neck.

CHAPTER 9

Each time the families gathered on the banks of the Euphrates River. From there, everyone could see Eden. It was a land of wonder, and as each year went on, it was slowly becoming a land of myth and legend. But each year, they returned to remember, tell stories, celebrate, and meet with the Designer. Adam and Eve were there. Abel's wife, Miriam, and Cain's family were all present. Each year there were more people. It was a wonderful time.

I watched Abel bring his lamb before everyone. Then Cain drove his cart to the same meeting place. Abel greeted Cain as his brother and embraced him with love, which was always spilling from his heart. Cain, though, was indifferent. To me, it appeared Cain had a feast on his mind, and this gift-giving was a chore.

The cool of the evening had begun, and everyone waited for the familiar sound of the Designer walking through the fields to meet with them. The atmosphere was filled with expectation. It was something powerful when the family met with the Designer. Through all the whispering voices, I could hear His footsteps. My ears are keener than most, so I heard Him long before the people did. As He came closer, it was as if they felt Him before they could hear Him. Then there was His familiar whistling. The children sensed Him before the adults did. I could hear it in their voices. The parents could not stop the excitement when the Designer was near.

When He appeared, there was an eruption of joy. People were calling out to Him, and He would stop and connect with each one. He loved these people with everything He had, and they felt it. To each one, He spoke truth, and they encountered it as love and faithfulness. Even though some received His corrections, they too experienced it as love and joy. It is something that I never tire of seeing.

Finally, after what seemed an age, the Designer stood with Cain and Abel. Adam and Eve were nearby; they always loved to see their boys bring their best to the Designer. By this stage, Wisdom and I found a tree close enough to hear all that was being spoken to the brothers. The sense of excitement in Abel needed no words, and the sense of indifference in Cain also required no words—two brothers, yet so different.

Cain feigned enthusiasm by saying, "Let's do this so we can feast together with our families." I think he was also trying to distract the Designer so He would not look too closely at the wheat in the cart.

Abel said, "My Lord, my heart and my love is yours, and I am forever thankful for everything you have given me." I could see tears flowing down Abel's face. He was at one with the Designer, and the Designer was at one with Him.

The Designer said to him, "Well done, my friend; well done, my son." These words breathed life into Abel, and it seemed all of time could have stood still at that moment. All could see the light that glowed within Abel and were drawn to it.

All but one ...

The Designer turned to Cain and said, "Cain, my son, come sit with me. Place your hands into the soil. You have done so well; the ground has yielded a bountiful crop. You should be very proud of all that you have achieved. Now come, feel deeper than you have felt before."

Cain had been asked this before and had done this before. He believed he knew the right things to say and do. Initially, he even tried to copy Abel's words, making them his own. He'd seen how the Designer responded to his brother's words. Surely all he had to do was repeat them. The Designer listened, but there was not the joy I saw with Abel. I was seeing sadness. The Designer's heart was breaking, and he had allowed it to break each year. It hurt Him that Cain saw Him this way, interacting with Him as if this was just another duty. Everything within Him invited Cain to go deeper, beyond the sorrow, disappointment, and loneliness, into His love, His healing love. But the pain overwhelmed Cain's desire to discover such love each time.

Both had brought gifts for the Designer, but like each year, He was more interested in them than the gifts. He could see their hearts long before He even considered their gifts. I watched as the Designer got up and approached Abel's lamb. Looking back at Abel, he smiled and said, "This could be the best one yet." Abel beamed, and the glow within him seemed to grow.

The Designer looked like He was going to Cain's cart, but He walked past it, glancing around as He passed. He was looking for someone in the crowd. Finally, when He couldn't find the person, He called out, "I am looking for Cain's apprentice. Can he please come forward?" I watched Cain as the Designer did this, and he had what appeared to be a smug smile on his face. He thought the apprentice was about to be blamed for the mildewed wheat.

The Designer waited. Finally, the young apprentice came forward. He was on the verge of tears, and I could see all he wanted to do was hide. He knew that he had disobeyed his master.

What happened next, though, shocked everyone. The Designer didn't call him 'apprentice'; He called him by his name. "Enoch. Come closer; I have something to give to you."

Everything went silent, as everyone wanted to see what the Designer was about to do.

"Enoch, I was there when you chose the best to place on the cart. I was there when you wrestled with right and wrong. I was the voice that reminded you of what friendship with me looks like. Enoch, you will live many years in this land. You will carry my light within you, and you will be forever known as my friend. I will show you things that no eye has ever seen or ear has heard. Enoch, I love you."

I spun back to look at Cain and saw he was seething. He knew the apprentice, who was also his son, had disobeyed him, and all he could think of was punishing him. Enoch would most likely receive what Cain believed he deserved. Cain slowly turned and fixed his glare on Abel. I shudder to imagine what Cain was thinking about Abel.

Turning back to the Designer, I saw the moment had not been lost on Him. I could see He was not angry with Cain but deeply sad. Cain pushed his way out of the crowd. He was angry, and no one was getting in his way. We all had seen him this way before. Usually, it took a few days for him to calm down and be himself again. I could see Abel wanted to follow him, but the Designer stopped him and said, "Leave him to me. I will go to him."

CHAPTER 10

I knew I needed to follow Cain, but everything within me wanted to be with the people and the celebration. So much life flowed when all the people came together to celebrate. I could smell the cooking from the fires all around me. Beautiful aromas were reaching up to the heavens. Something about the smell of bread baking overtakes all of my senses. Children were running in and out of the cooking area. Parents warned them of the dangers, but the children wanted to play and explore. This was a special day, and joy was lingering in the air.

I turned to see the Designer walking along the edge of the river, and I heard Him calling out to Cain. It reminded me of a time long ago when he did the same for Adam and Eve. He knew where Cain was, but it seemed Cain did not.

I flew on ahead and found Cain back in his workshop. Things were flying in all directions. He was making a loud noise. No one else was there; they were all off celebrating. This seemed to fuel his anger, and I could see he would not be soothed any time soon.

The Designer came and sat outside the workshop. He had always known where Cain was, and he just sat and waited. He was not upset or angry; if anything, He was listening to the sounds of celebration drifting across the fields. Every now and then, a cheer would go up, and then it would go back to chatter and squeals of laughter from the children. He truly loved these people.

Minutes of waiting soon turned into hours, and yet the Designer still waited. He was in no rush and knew it would have been a waste of time to go in when Cain was so angry. The Designer spotted me up in the tree and came over to me. I loved it when He would do this. He always made time for me.

"Eagle, what have you seen today?" He asked.

"My Lord, I have seen many things, and some have thrilled my heart, and some have saddened me," I said.

"Tell me of the things that have thrilled your heart, Eagle. I always love to hear what causes you to fly higher," he said with a smile.

"My Lord, today I soared with Wisdom. She is so beautiful, and I love soaring with her."

"That is because Eagle, she was made to soar with you. Did you not know this?"

This shocked me. Did I know this? Had I always known this? Something came alive in me just asking me this question, and I said, "It had always felt as if we were one when we soared together, my Lord."

"Yes, Eagle. It is true. She was made for you. She is like you, but she carries a wisdom you do not. Just like you carry an understanding she does not," He said. "She carries knowledge of future events and has seen much. But when you are together, you both see and feel much more. So, tell me, Eagle, what have you seen today?"

"My Lord, I saw two snakes. One was alive and talked like the strange lizard in Eden. The other was dead, and I was unsure if it had spoken or not. The one that was alive sat on the cart beside Cain. I could hear its evil whispers, and every one of them reminded me of the voice that had spoken to Eve in Eden. I will never forget that voice. It was harsh, and it was horrible."

"Yes, Eagle, I saw them too. The one that you saw dead had actually spoken. It had told Abel how good he was, indeed how much better he was than Cain. It spoke of Cain's jealousy towards him. It even told Abel that he would have been a far better farmer than Cain."

I've occasionally heard the Designer chuckle, and this was another one of those times. It was like He was playing out the events in His head and seeing the snake's words fall short of Abel's ears.

"My Lord, I saw Abel's footprint on the snake's neck from when he had killed it. Why could Abel see through the voice clearly and Cain could not?"

"That is because Abel knows my presence. He knows my voice and has clung to every word I have spoken." He paused before He continued, "He reminds me of Adam from before he ate from *The Tree of Knowledge of Good and Bad*. Adam also loved my voice, and this was precious to me. There were times he would ask me to repeat myself again and again, and he did not want to miss a word. He cherished every word I gave him and clung to it. How often have you seen him sitting with me out by the river, Eagle?"

"Many, many times, my Lord. More times than I could count. Sometimes he did not even come home in the evening. He would linger where you met him, and no one could disturb him."

This made the Designer smile. He loved it when others could see what His presence could do for His creation. I have seen people be healed, broken bones restored, and sicknesses flee simply by being near His presence.

"Each time Abel would meet with me, I would invite him to press his fingers into the ground. Much like I did with you, Eagle.

Each time, he would move beyond the surface and connect with the love that flows through all things. He no longer felt the sorrow, the shame, or the loneliness of the past, for he had healed." The Designer paused and exhaled gently before continuing, "I would share my heart with him. He knows things that no one else could possibly have learned in their time on the earth. I trust him with these mysteries, much like I trust you with them, Eagle."

Did the Designer just say that He trusts me? This was more than I could comprehend. I knew He loved me, and I felt it in my bones. But, He said He trusts me. The Designer trusts me.

"My Lord, I have no words to express what this means to me. I have known your love every day of my life. To have your trust, though, is beyond my comprehension."

"It is my joy to share my trust with you, Eagle. I long to share it with everyone, and today you saw me share it with Abel and Enoch," He said.

There was a long moment of silence. I wanted to sit in what the Designer had just said to me and linger in His words. But we had been waiting outside of Cain's noisy workshop. What was happening inside now was unknown; everything had gone quiet. We could still hear the noises of the celebrations and smell the food cooking. Something again was bothering me.

"Eagle, you have a question for me," He said.

"Yes, Lord, I do," I replied. "They are brothers who look so much alike but behave so differently. They were born in the same home and raised by the same parents. How is it that they are so different?"

"Eagle, there are some similarities, and they are both loved by their parents and me," He said. "They are also very unique. Look around you, Eagle. Have you ever noticed two people who were the same?"

"No, my Lord. There is no one the same," I replied.

"This is of my design," He said. "Each person is as different as the next, and each one is designed by me and known by me. They each love differently, think differently, and behave differently."

"The same parents raised these two brothers, but they have developed totally different ways of looking at the world. Cain is a thinker and problem-solver, and Abel carries great empathy and is a peacemaker," He continued, "What they do with their design is totally up to them. Remember, to each I have given choice, which I will never take from them. To do so is to stop loving them."

I sat and pondered this for a time. The Designer knew more questions were coming, so He waited for me. "My Lord, how deeply did Adam and Eve's shame affect the two brothers?"

"Very deeply," He replied. "It changed them."

I pondered more on this. I had seen the change with my own eyes. Even on that fateful day, I had seen them go from brothers to competitors, and they hadn't even touched the *tree*.

"Adam and Eve's shame went for many years unhealed. Even to this day, there are times they talk of it as I walk with them along the banks of the river. They long to be back on the other side of the river and in Eden. They desire to no longer hide in the clothes I made for them, and they want to be forever free of the shame they walk in. The two brothers inherited the shame simply because Adam and Eve did not choose to be healed. It was their way of protecting themselves from having to feel it."

Again, I remembered back to the moment the Designer had invited me to sit under *The Tree of Life* and be healed of the shame I carried. I had wanted to cast aside what the Designer had asked me to do and kill the strange lizard to be rid of its voice. When the Designer invited me to sit with Him, I couldn't even look Him in the eye. I felt I had abandoned him, disappointed him, and broken His heart. Maybe I did all of those things, but He has never spoken about it. What He did say was that He loved me. Every single time I have heard Him speak, I have heard this in His words, even if those were not words He had spoken. When I sat under *The Tree of Life*, He invited me to go beyond my pain and into His love. It was only in His love that I felt released from my shame.

The Designer's voice broke me out of pondering as if He was reading my mind, "Eagle, each time that voice of shame tries to speak to you, I am here inviting you to *The Tree of Life*. Did you know that?"

"My Lord, the pathway to that *tree* is shut. The angels you placed there would not let me go there, even if I tried. How can I go back there?"

I always loved it when the Designer would touch me, and at that moment, he touched my head and said, "I have told you this before, but I will tell you again, your mind is like a library of events, and you can go to any of them whenever you want. Your mind will carry you there and can show you even more than you comprehended when you were there, and it might even show you more than a dead tree."

That dead tree ...

"No one can take these memories from you, Eagle, and no one can prevent you from being there. You touched my love, and that is eternal. It is the same love you touched under that *tree* as you touch it today. It contains the same power and the same healing that you encountered there. Eagle, hear me well; nothing can separate you from my love, nothing."

CHAPTER 11

All I wanted to do was linger in that moment.

When the Designer speaks of love, I feel the atmosphere around me shimmer. I know I do not hear just words; I am actually feeling a power that creates and restores. My mind races through every encounter where I have felt this phenomenon. It has happened more times than I can remember, and tonight it happened again.

He spoke words of my identity. He spoke words of His trust in me. He spoke the words of the one who soars beside me. He has allowed me to see what many call the mysteries of the Designer.

The very first moment of my conscious memory was sitting on His arm. I do not know how old I was, but I was young, and Eden was enormous. I remember the day He presented me to Adam. Adam looked into my eyes and simply called me Eagle, which is what I have been called ever since. But to know me is to know more than my name; it's to see my character. Tonight, when the Designer said that He trusts me ... well ... all I can say is that I felt seen. He didn't remind me of failures. He spoke my restoration.

Tonight, as I sit in this tree outside the house of a man who is out of control, I can still feel the Designer's love. There is pain, torment, dejection, and raw anger inside that house, and it is so close to me. The love I feel is greater than all of these things. The love I feel can calm the anger, lift Cain out of dejection and torment, and heal. It is all right here within his grasp.

However, for this to be a love story, Cain needs to choose this love. He needs to believe in this love. If he seeks it, all these things will be added to him.

So, tonight ... we wait ...

CHAPTER 12

It is late, and the Designer has built a fire. The celebrations have long since quieted, and the smell of cooking is no longer drifting across the fields. All is quiet ... even Cain.

Tonight the Designer seems troubled. Since talking with me, He has not said a thing; He just tended to the fire. It's not an overly cold night, but the air is cool, and He is sitting transfixed by the fire and lost in His own thoughts. The longer He waits for Cain to come out, the more it seems His thoughts are becoming unsettled. These are the times I wished I knew what to say to comfort Him, and I had no words, so I waited with Him.

Deep in the night, the door to the workshop opened, and I could see the silhouette of Cain. He must have had a fire going from the light glowing behind him. Initially, I couldn't see his face, but as he came closer to the Designer's fire, what I saw scared me. I think I expected Cain to have calmed down and come to his senses, but the look on his face was cold. He was still angry, and much like the fire behind him, he was ablaze with a force that caused even his dog to cower away.

The power of this force did nothing to the Designer, and He didn't flinch or react to Cain's anger. He simply looked up and said, "Cain, come and sit with me by the fire. I'd like to talk with you."

Cain looked in no mood to be sitting around a fire and talking with the Designer, but something in His voice drew Cain toward Him. Once he was seated, there was more silence, and all that could be heard was the crackle of the fire and the Designer poking at it with a stick.

Finally, Cain broke the silence and said, "What do you want?"

Without looking at Cain and still gazing into the fire, He asked, "Why are you so dejected?" The silence was the only thing that responded to Him. So, He sat a little longer with Cain. The Designer spoke again when it became apparent Cain wouldn't respond. "Why are you jealous of Abel? Do you think He has been accepted by me and you have not?"

Cain bristled at that but still said nothing. I could feel the rage within him, and he was keeping it bottled up inside.

"Cain, do you remember the day when your parents ate from *The Tree of Knowledge of Good and Bad*? That day you and Abel had found a beautiful waterhole. I made that waterhole for you. I knew how much you loved diving in and searching for everything beneath the surface. Everything about that waterhole was designed for you. I was there that day, and when I saw the wonder on your face at what you had discovered, my heart sang. So happy were you to find it, you were running back to find your parents to tell them about it. But something happened that day that changed your entire world. You felt it in the bond with your brother even then. It was that day you started to shift from brothers to competitors. Do you remember that you got into a scuffle? You both fell and scraped up your elbows. But such was your determination to get to your parents first; you didn't even notice.

Do you remember the confusion when you returned to where they should have been and you could not find them? You were so young back then, and many different emotions flowed through your body. You discovered what they had done, but something else shifted for you as well when they hid what they had done. Mistakes are not designed to be hidden but to learn from. When we hide from our mistakes, shame has a much greater opportunity to invade every area of our thoughts."

Cain had softened a little, and I saw his shoulders slump. He was tired, and the anger within him slowly began to ebb away. It was then the Designer turned to him, looked him in the eyes, and said, "Abel's relationship with me is not based on what he can do; it's grounded in the love he has for me and the love I have for him. It is the same love I have for you."

Once again, the Designer turned back to the fire and started poking it with the stick. Time passed, and He got up and added more wood to the fire. It is evident that He was not going anywhere soon. Once He was satisfied with the fire, he turned back to Cain, but I could see the pain in the Designer's eyes this time. It was dark, and His face flickered with the firelight, but I think I saw tears filling His eyes. When He spoke, I could feel the heartbreak in His voice.

"Cain, the anger you carry will give birth to something you will not be able to control. Don't let it take over your mind and poison your heart. You are a good man, and I love you very much."

After a short while, the Designer got up from the fire. Cain was looking at the dirt and did not even look to see the Designer move away from the fire. He was like a statue sitting there. He was still in that position when the sun came up. I watched as he stirred. His face was filthy from the smoke and distorted from the anger that had consumed him all night. He got up and moved away from the smoking embers, and under his breath, I heard him spit out the words, "He loves me." They were not spoken with affection but contempt.

Once he was back in his home, I was about to stretch my wings out to take flight. I had been sitting in one position all night, and all I wanted to do was to fly to feel the cool wind of the morning and the sun on my face. But before I could, a movement to the left caught my eye. That same snake coiled up beside Cain on the cart was in the tree with me. I have never been scared of another animal in my life, but this animal was contorted and looked every bit like the strange lizard in Eden. It launched its whole body at me with its fangs bared. It was trying to strike my wing. In the split second of seeing it and it launching at me, I grabbed its neck with my talons and threw it to the ground. It hissed up at me and spoke with that familiar twisted and evil voice, "He's mine," and then slithered away.

I had seen enough here. It was time to fly. I needed to find Wisdom.

CHAPTER 13

"Wisdom, something is wrong."

"Yes, Eagle, I have felt it too," she said.

"What should we do?"

"Should?" she responded.

Her answer surprised me, but I have learned by now that this is the time for me to listen and not speak.

"Eagle, there are many things we could do right now, but what we 'should' do is a different question." She continued, "When we use the word 'should', we are trying to read someone's mind and then act from what we have assumed. It's a fool's errand. No, Eagle, this word 'should' is not one that we should be using."

I could hear Wisdom laughing under her breath at her own joke, but I could see what she meant. In my mind, the snake needed to die, and I needed to follow Cain to see who his anger would affect next. Then, I would go to someone who could fix whatever his anger was about to do. All the while hoping I was not too late. Thinking about all of this made me tired. Yes, the word 'should' was a problem.

"So, if there is nothing we 'should' do. What do you think we could do?" Now it was my turn to laugh at my own use of words.

Wisdom smiled at me and exclaimed, "Today, we soar."

And at that, she plummeted towards the ground with such speed. I love watching her do this. She was hunting for a wind that will take her higher. Every part of her senses is awake to this, and as an eagle, we never feel more alive than when we hunt for the wind to take us higher so we can ride the thermals. From up there, we can see far and wide. The Designer made us with eyes to see beyond any other animal or person, and today we are using them to discover more of the beauty of His creation.

From up there, we could see back into Eden. We were allowed to fly over Eden, but I no longer thought we could approach the *two trees* still growing in the heart of Eden. We could see they both thrived, and the angels still guarded *The Tree of Life*. A pang of sorrow went through my heart when I looked upon those *trees*. So many days, weeks, months, and years were lived around them. Every part of my being longed to be back there, sitting in *The Tree of Life* with Wisdom and feasting on the fruit.

It was then that I noticed the Designer walking among the *two trees*. It looked like He was in a deep discussion with himself. He was all alone, and it broke my heart to see him like this. He designed us to love each other, and He had designed us to love Him. Wisdom saw Him too and said, "Come Eagle, the Designer needs this time to think. Some decisions we make need to be made by us and us alone."

Although I did not understand what Wisdom was saying, I knew she had foresight, which seemed to be bothering her. When she is unsettled, she loves to fly and explore. Once again, she dived towards the earth and found the wind she was looking for, and before I knew it, she was so high in the sky. Now it was my turn. Like her, I tucked my wings in and flew as fast as possible until

I found the wind. To find it brings such joy, as I did, I unfurled my wings and took to the heavens. All day we did this. Further and further from Eden we flew. At times we perched on the rocky crags of high mountains to catch our breath, and once we had, we tucked our wings back in and plummeted towards the earth again in search of the next wind. Up there, we were free. We were away from all the concerns of people. We were able to be present, and we were able to be together.

"Together," I said to Wisdom. "As we were flying, this word would not leave my mind. Can we talk about it?"

"Yes, Eagle. What is your question?"

"Back in Eden, the Designer could see that Adam was alone. He brought every animal to Adam, and we got our names from him. But none of us could fill the role that was missing for Adam. He was alone, and the Designer told him of this loneliness."

"Yes, I remember that day well, Eagle. There was something within me that wanted to be the one who cured Adam's loneliness, but it was not to be," she said.

"Wisdom, when we are together, I feel a sense of power that is far greater. It's like it was meant to be that way. I feel like we can do infinitely more together than apart. Do you understand what I'm saying?"

"Yes, Eagle, I do. I have been waiting for you to understand this. We were never meant to do life alone."

Then she said, "Eagle, many years from now, people will hear the story of Eve's creation and think she was the only one created for Adam. They will call this 'marriage', but I don't think this was the Designer's only intention. He wanted us all to find that connection in all that surrounds us. It is what you speak of with the strength of connection that you feel. He calls this 'unity'. It is what happens when we love each other well."

"So, Wisdom, is this why I feel so troubled?"

"Yes, Eagle, it is. You are feeling the fracturing of a relationship. Unity is breaking; whatever happens next will happen from Cain's choices. These choices we are not allowed to intervene in."

That sounded ominous to me. Cain's anger frightened me and caused me to experience new emotions.

"Wisdom, when I sat in the tree outside Cain's workshop, a talking snake struck at me. I believe it wanted to kill me. I felt emotions I had not felt before. I felt the shock of an animal attacking me. I felt the reaction within me to protect myself, and once again, I felt the desire to destroy the snake."

"Yes, Eagle, things are changing."

We were silent for a time and allowed ourselves to hang in the wind. From the ground, it must look like we are going nowhere, but to us, it is one of our design features. It is a joy to do.

I was deep in these thoughts when Wisdom abruptly interrupted me, saying, "Come Eagle, something terrible has happened."

CHAPTER 14

The scene that greeted us will be etched into my mind for all eternity; it was horrifying. Abel was dead.

When something so terrible happens, it is easy to look for another outcome or even believe that this cannot be. But Abel was lying as still as the snake he had trod on. There was no movement, no breath in his lungs, no glow, and no longer a smile on his face. Nothing about this picture looked right; everything about it looked wrong.

People were panicking. I could hear a woman screaming and then saw her burst out of a home and run towards the still form of Abel on the ground. It was Abel's wife, Miriam, and she could not be calmed. Her wailing was so loud that people from every corner of the settlement came running toward them. She was cradling Abel in her arms and was soon covered in his blood. The blood had stopped flowing, but there was just so much. I couldn't believe there had been so much blood contained in one body, Abel's body.

There was nothing that Wisdom, nor I, could do. We were utterly helpless. Around Miriam, there was pandemonium; no one could believe what they were seeing. It was like a bad dream that we could not wake up from.

Where was the Designer? He should be here. Surely He could do something about this. Surely He could heal this wound. Surely He could bring Abel back to us. I determined in my heart that I would get the Designer and have Him fix this bad dream. Just as I was about to fly, it was Wisdom again who simply said, "This is not yours to fix, Eagle. Only the Designer knows what needs to happen next. Never before has anything like this happened, and now the Designer will show us the path forward."

"But where is He Wisdom! He could have prevented this," I screamed back. "If only He had been here, then Abel would still be alive."

Wisdom didn't speak again. She, too, was deeply grieved and pained by what she saw. Even with the power of foresight and the intuition that this would happen, witnessing this horrific scene, I could see, affected her so deeply.

Then to my left, I heard another scream, again it was from a woman. I turned, but I already knew who it would be … it was Eve. She is the most beautiful of women, but at this moment, she cared nothing about what people saw. Once again, I witnessed the power of unbridled grief. I have heard few more raw sounds than this in my lifetime, and today I have now heard it twice.

Eve has changed since leaving Eden. Every now and then, I can see the joy she and Adam shared in Eden, but often I see her sitting on the banks of the Euphrates, staring into Eden. Sometimes the Designer meets her there, and I don't dare go close to them when they are talking. It's a sacred space only the two of them share. The thing about Eve that hasn't changed, though, is her passion for her sons. She loves them with everything she has. She is their greatest cheerleader, and she is always telling everyone about how good her sons are. But now, their mother was distraught.

Eve joined Miriam and held them both. Son, she too was covered in her son's blood. She was wailing at the sky and rocking back and forth. It was too much for me to bear to watch; no parent should have to face this. She ignored everyone that gathered around them. People were confused and saying things to her, but she heard none of them. She only saw the lifeless form of her son in her arms. She spoke to him, telling him to wake up and open his eyes. It was the most hopeless thing I have ever seen. I would have sooner relived the exit from Eden than to witness this.

As I turned my face away from the scene, I saw Adam. I do not know how long he had been standing there, but it was like his legs were stone. He was paralyzed with shock by what he was seeing. Adam is always a warm man. He carries himself well, and his leadership has been invaluable since leaving Eden, but now, he is as motionless as Abel.

I watched him closely, and I could see grief giving way to anger. Adam could see that this was no accident. The weapon everyone had overlooked still lay in a pool of blood beside Eve. This was not a shepherd's tool; it was a farmer's tool. I watched as Adam's eyes widened at the realization of whose tool it was ... one son lay dead on the ground, and the other son's digging tool lay beside him in his blood. Adam's eyes closed, and tears started flowing down his face. Like Eve, he no longer cared who saw his grief.

I watched as Adam approached the scene. I expected him to go straight to Eve and hold her, but he did not. He went and grabbed the tool, appearing to hide it from Eve's eyes. At that moment, I could once again see the leader in Adam. At that moment, he wanted to protect Eve from a double portion of loss and grief.

After throwing the tool away, he rushed to Eve's side and held her. Eve turned from Abel and into Adam's arms, but instead of hugging him, she yelled, "Where were you? Why weren't you here to save our son? You should have been here?"

Slowly her accusations and strikes got less and less as she gave herself over to her grief again. She collapsed on his chest, and Adam picked her up and held her close. His tears and her tears mingled together. So raw was the grief that people turned away from them to give them this moment together. Eve was covered in Abel's blood, and soon Adam was as well, but it mattered not to either of them. They believed life flowed through the blood, and now, at least, they could wear the life their son had carried.

I bowed my head. I, too, could no longer watch. The tears burned as they flowed from my eyes. Not in my wildest imagination had I believed I would be seeing this today. I loved Abel ... Everyone loved Abel.

CHAPTER 15

"Where's Cain?" I heard someone yell. "Someone must find Cain and tell him what has happened to his brother." I could not tell whose voice it was. There were so many people around, and they all seemed to think this was the best thing to do. No one knew what to say to Adam and Eve or Miriam, so everyone scattered, looking for Cain. Deep inside, I knew Cain would not be found. Sooner or later, the tool Adam had disposed of would be found, and people would be looking for who did this.

Cain knew these lands too well. Ever since they left Eden, Cain would often be off looking for new ground. Sometimes he would be gone for days on his adventures and then turn up acting as if he had only been gone for a few hours. Eve would often worry about him, but he always turned up again; of this, he would always remind her.

Everyone had now left except for Abel's parents and his wife, Miriam. The wailing had ceased, and now there were just tears. Miriam could not stop saying, "No, you can't be gone." Eve had gone deathly silent, and Adam did his best to comfort them both while pressing down his grief and the growing sense of loss.

I had once asked Adam what he felt when he walked out of Eden. He told me that, at first, he felt utterly empty. He spoke of needing to make a raft to get his family across the Euphrates River, and while he built the raft, the emptiness left him. But once he pushed off from Eden's bank, that emptiness returned and never really left.

I had even worked up enough courage to ask him if he still blamed Eve for eating the fruit from *The Tree of Knowledge of Good and Bad.* He was silent for so long that I thought he would not answer me, but eventually, he did. He was wrestling with the words to say. He loved Eve with his entire life.

He said, "I did blame her, and I was wrong too. I did not know what to say, and I did not want to disappoint the Designer. I have always sought to please him. That day, Eagle, I discovered something new about Him; He didn't want to be pleased; He wanted to be loved."

I remember that conversation so clearly. It was another moment when time seemed to slow down, and one of the mysteries of the Designer was revealed.

Adam continued, but this time in a whisper that spoke of the depth of his pain, "I blamed her, but I was there. I was not right beside her, but I was near enough to see her by that *tree*. That *tree* intrigued us both. Some days, it even seemed to call to us. That strange lizard spoke to us many times before that fateful day. Some days I was strong for Eve; other days, she was strong for me. On our best days, I could see how united and powerful we were together. It only took one day, when we were both weak and separated, for things to unravel ... So, do I blame her now? No, Eagle, I do not. Do I wish we could have that time again?" he asked rhetorically. "Yes, Eagle, I do." He paused in thought, then finally said, "To this day, I cannot believe that I allowed myself to be taken in by a voice questioning the love of the Designer. Not a day goes by without me thinking of that choice. I should have clung to every word of the Designer."

After a time, he turned to me and said, "Eagle, you have felt the power of His words; how could I have been so easily fooled?"

It was strange this conversation returned to me as I sat with the trio in this brutal and painful moment. I knew that Adam would have greater grief to face and more choices to come that would affect the family which was growing around them.

As I pondered all of this, I had not noticed the Designer was standing right next to Wisdom. They were in deep discussion. He spoke a word to her, and she took flight and headed west. The Designer looked at me, and I could see that He had been crying. Seeing His tears broke my heart again. This had affected Him more than I could bear. Watching His tears was tearing more at my spirit. The Designer was in turmoil, as well. His heart was broken.

He then went and sat in the dirt and blood with Adam, Eve, and Miriam. There were few words and many tears.

CHAPTER 16

I watched the Designer sitting on the ground with Abel and witnessed something I had never seen Him do before. Many years ago, when He sat with me under *The Tree of Life*, He invited me to let my talons go deep into the ground, past the sorrow, the disappointment, and loneliness, and into His love. Now I was watching Him do the same. This time, however, the dirt was mixed with Abel's blood, and it was also mixed with Miriam's, Eve's, Adam's, and His tears. Never before had the dirt received such an extraordinary and painful sacrifice.

All those years ago, Wisdom told me of the great love story that would continue long after Eve had eaten the fruit from the wrong *tree*. She was hopeful, and she encouraged me not to lose hope and not turn away. Somehow, this time, I struggled to find hope, and I tasted the bitter taste of death again.

My animal friends in Eden who gave up their lives so Adam and his family could be clothed was painful to witness. This, though, seemed impossible to fathom. This was no sacrifice; this was death taken, not death given. This was senseless, and this seemed utterly pointless. The only result I could see was loss; there was nothing here to gain.

I was in Eden when the Designer said to Adam, "You may freely eat from every tree in Eden, except *The Tree of Knowledge of Good and Bad*. If you eat its fruit, you are sure to die." These words were now ringing in my ears, "sure to die." What had that *tree* done to us? Here I sit and watch the hearts of Abel's parents, his wife, and the Designer in agony. It was harsh and brutal, and there was no turning back from this moment.

I had questions, but this was not the time to ask. Wisdom was gone, and the Designer was grieving. Surely this cannot be the end of Abel. Surely there must be more. His whole life is now reduced to an empty body, and all his blood poured out on into the ground.

Another memory came to my mind; this time, it was when the Designer was speaking to Adam before He closed Eden. He said, "By the sweat of your brow will you have food to eat until you return to the ground from which you were made. For you were made from dust, and dust you will return." Was this what the Designer was talking about? Had he already seen what would befall those created in His own image? Surely this is not the end.

It was now late into the evening, and the Designer was talking softly to Adam, Eve, and Miriam. I could hear something about a cave and something about a safe place to put Abel's body for all time. Eve was not ready to move him. Miriam looked tired beyond what was humanly possible and did not want to leave this blood-soaked spot. Adam kept looking over to where he threw the farmer's digging tool.

The Designer stood up and went to each of them. To Miriam, he touched her heart and spoke of the husband that Abel is to her. He then went to Adam and Eve and spoke to them of the son that he is to them both. There was something about what He said that caught my attention. He did not say the husband he 'was' or the son he 'was.' He spoke about the man who 'is' as if he was still alive. It was an odd moment, but I knew that the Designer never spoke a word that was a lie, and everything He spoke had life. I was intrigued and felt a flicker of hope, once again, start to burn within my chest. Wisdom was not even here for me to ask her. Maybe she would know what the Designer meant. It was, yet again, another question that I tucked away to ask when I could.

The Designer then asked for permission to take Abel's body to the cave He had spoken about. It seemed odd to me that a cave would become an eternal resting place, but I had no idea what would become of Abel's body. Each of them trusted the Designer; they knew He loved Abel and would honor him. Each of them came to Abel, reached out, and touched him in a way of farewelling him. Eve ran her hands over his head. Still, the tears flowed. She had raised Abel and cleaned the dirt from his face many times. I could sense each of those times came back into her mind as she reached out to him. Many of those memories were good ones, and as each one touched her, a peace settled on her. Adam came forward and once again picked Abel up and held him. This would be the last time he would hold his son. Up until then, Adam had kept his emotions quietly to himself, but now he opened his mouth and roared at the stars. I am certain everyone in the community heard it. It was raw and mixed with love, grief, and anger, I am sure. After a time, he lowered Abel to the ground and went to Eve. They held each other tight, knowing that this pain would never heal.

Miriam was last to come forward. All of her tears had been cried out. She had roared at the sky earlier, but now she was tender, just as Abel was tender with her. They had never had a child, and right now, that loss must have been so hard to hold. She must have been thinking this as I saw her hold her belly and cry. This was the last time she would see him, and the way she held Abel was too precious for me to watch, so I turned away. This was the moment of two lovers and was for them alone.

Abel was a man to look up to. Other couples would look to Abel and Miriam for wisdom and advice. He was a man who knew the love of the Designer flowed through his veins. He would talk to everyone about this love as if it were a pearl of great value. One day I heard a man question that love. Abel merely smiled and said, "Sir, think of it this way. If you found a treasure in a field, would you not sell everything to purchase that field so that you would possess that treasure?"

The man responded, "Of course, I would. That treasure would be all I needed to live."

"Exactly," exclaimed Abel. "This love is the very thing you seek; it is all you need to live." He then continued, "Everything else can be earned by the work of your hands, but not this love. It is not earned; this love is a given."

Everyone who met Abel received this gift of love; he withheld it from no one. It did not matter if you were young or old or if you were an apprentice or a leader of people. Abel loved as the Designer had loved him.

What I saw next was difficult to understand, but it is what I saw. The Designer would not rush Miriam; He waited until she was ready. Through tears again, Miriam farewelled Abel. Then the Designer lifted Abel from the ground and walked off toward the Euphrates River. At first, I thought that he was going to wash Abel. But as he approached the river, instead of stepping into the water, He walked straight across it and into Eden. No one had been there since Adam and Eve left with their family. This I had to see, so I took to the air and followed the Designer into Eden. Although I could not approach *The Tree of Life*, I could sit in a tree that allowed me to see what happened. There he lowered Abel onto the ground by *The Tree of Life*. Many times I had seen Abel glow after He had been with the Designer, but this time I watched that same glow grow within him. Then the most extraordinary thing happened. That glow, although translucent, formed a man.

It was beautiful and looked like the sun in human form. Abel's body lay still on the ground, but this spirit man rose and embraced the Designer. Abel lived! I wanted to scream it out loud. I wanted to fly to Miriam and tell her that her husband lived.

But before I could, Wisdom flew down beside me. I pointed at Abel, and joy filled my voice, "He's alive," I said, "Abel is alive!"

"Yes," said Wisdom, "but it is not what you think," she continued. "See, Abel's body still lies on the ground, and that body will soon become the dust Adam was made from. What you see is Abel's spirit, and that spirit, Eagle, is something death cannot touch. Abel is now forever with the Designer right here in Eden."

This day had brought with it so many new and different emotions, but this was another one I could not even fathom. "Abel had a spirit?" I said to Wisdom. "So, Wisdom, his life was not in his blood, but his spirit?"

Wisdom just smiled at me and said, "There is much for you to learn yet, Eagle, but think of it this way: the body needs blood, and without it, the body will die. So yes, there is life in the blood; it powers the body. However, it is Abel's spirit that you know. It is his spirit that loved as the Designer loved him. It is his spirit that loved Miriam, Adam, and Eve. His spirit is who he is; as I said, death cannot claim his spirit, like the way the ground claimed his blood."

So, Abel lived ...

CHAPTER 11

The Designer carefully wrapped Abel's body, and just like he had said to Miriam, He would take it and seal it in a cave where no further harm could come to him.

Wisdom and I took flight and circled over Eden, watching this extraordinary event unfold. To the rest of creation, it appeared as if nothing had happened. Faraway, we could see people were again going about their work, and the animals of the forest were foraging for meals or building nests to care for their families. We could also see Adam, Eve, and Miriam all together, sitting around a fire.

We saw the Designer look up at us, and as He did, He called us to come to Him. This was an equally extraordinary moment; we were about to witness something that had not happened before.

We landed in a tree near the Designer. It is hard to describe the feelings I felt being back there. The smells, the familiar mountains, trees, waterholes, and the *two trees* in the center of Eden were all there. Memories came flooding back to me like energetic fire flowing through every sinew and muscle of my body. I never wanted to leave.

The Designer could see I was overwhelmed, and through the most calming smile, He welcomed me back to Eden, saying, "Eagle, there are things here that I want you to see. I know that you have many questions, but for the moment, I want you to see more of my creation. It is beyond anything you could imagine. Many will desire to see this in the days to come. For you are about to see eternity."

Wisdom was right beside me, and although she had foresight, I was certain that this was beyond what even she had seen. I heard her whisper, "What no eye has seen or ear has heard." There was a reverent awe in her voice. We were in a sacred moment.

Abel's lifeless body was wrapped on the ground, and I could no longer see him or the horrible wound on his head. That was both a sadness and a relief for me. I was sad as I would no longer be able to look on his face, and I felt relief simply because I did not want to remember the devastating blow that ended his life.

The glowing light that came from Abel was still there, as well. It was hard to even know what to do with this. I now knew that the glowing light was the very essence of Abel, but his wrapped body that lay apart from him made this whole scene so confusing to me. The glowing form of Abel felt very familiar to me. I could once again sense his love for me, and as I concentrated on him, I could easily recall all the memories and conversations we shared.

One of those memories that came flooding back to me was a day when Abel was sitting on a hill watching over his sheep. He saw me in the sky and motioned for me to come and sit beside him. Seeing an eagle and a man sitting and talking together must have been a sight.

He said, "Eagle, can you see that sheep down there? The one second from the left? It's got two black spots on it."

"Yes," I said.

He then said, "Watch this." At that, he called out the name, "yee-khoo-DEE." At that, the spotted sheep picked up its head and came straight to Abel. It not only knew his voice, it knew its name.

I asked Abel, "What does its name mean?"

He smiled and said, "Unique, for she is truly unique to me."

He then said, "Eagle, you have been tasked to watch over all things. It is a wonderful task to be given. But, Eagle, can you see all things?"

His question surprised me, as initially, I did not know the difference between what he asked. Surely what I could watch, I could clearly see.

Abel continued, "When you landed here, you saw many sheep. To the newcomer, they all look the same because we often look for purpose rather than their identity. So when you saw the sheep, you may have thought of how many people these sheep could clothe. Or perhaps you thought of how the milk they provide could also be used by many. However, you didn't realize this sheep had a name." He said as he continued to stroke the sheep.

I sat and pondered this for a long time. What he had said to me that day had weight, and I needed time to process it. Each word contained so much truth, but I could feel more than truth in Abel. I could feel his love for each animal in his care and also for me. I could feel the tears flowing again when I realized he was caring for me. He had given me one of the greatest lessons of my life: I was tasked to watch, but had I seen?

Today, once again, the Designer had asked me to watch, but now Abel's words were ringing in my ears ... what was I seeing?

The Designer had been kneeling for a long time beside the wrapped body of Abel. This was another sacred moment when time was irrelevant. It looked like the Designer was doing precisely what I had just done; he was reliving all the moments of the love they had shared. His tears naturally flowed at this moment, as did Wisdom's and mine.

It was then I felt He had given me a window into His soul. The Designer could literally do anything He wanted at that moment. If He desired it, He could have recreated Abel from the very dust He had used to make Adam. He could place Abel's glowing presence into that body and send him back to His family, but He didn't. Instead, He grieved. He had so many memories He could relive. From sitting with Abel by the banks of the Euphrates River to teaching him all he needed to know about sheep, to simply laughing with him in the cool of the evening. I was there for many of those memories, and if I relived just the ones I had, we would have been there for days. This was not a time to be rushed. Nor was it a time to merely watch; it was a time to see.

The glowing form of Abel slowly moved toward the Designer. He, too, was careful not to interrupt this moment, but as he slowly approached the Designer, a beautiful moment unfolded in front of Wisdom and me. The Designer had looked up at the angels guarding *The Tree of Life* and asked them to put away their flaming swords. At first, they appeared to not know why, but then it became clear, Abel was about to eat from the *tree*. The Designer simply smiled and nodded His permission to Abel. I stunning vision opened up in front of us. As Abel ate the fruit, the Designer and he became one. He was in the Designer, and the Designer was in Abel. Wisdom and I could barely breathe; such was the awe of this moment. Who would believe us if we spoke of what we had seen? The two had become one.

Even the angels appeared shocked by this. What had we all just witnessed? None of us uttered a word, and none of us wanted to disturb the enormity of this moment. We were witnessing eternity.

The Designer rose, picked up the wrapped form of Abel on the ground, and carried him into the wooded area just beyond *The Tree of Life*. As He did, the angels unsheathed their flaming swords again. He beckoned for us to follow Him. Wisdom and I were still so shocked it took a few moments for us to break from what we had just seen. We both looked at each other and tried to speak, but no words would form. Truly, what words were there to adequately describe what we witnessed?

We took flight just as the Designer slipped from view. Wisdom knew where He was going, and when she could finally form words, she said, "When the Designer told me to go east, He told me to prepare the cave to receive Abel's body. Come, I will show you the way."

We flew deep into Eden. When we got there, I could see a cave bigger than a man, but not large. It was large enough to possibly fit two or three men. Wisdom had cleaned it out, and it stood ready for Abel's body.

The Designer carried Abel with such honor and care. Even in death, knowing that Abel's spirit had left the body, He carried him as if he were still alive. To witness the magnitude of the Designer's grief was to witness the magnitude of His love for Abel. His love was powerful; I could feel it in the air.

He placed Abel's body in the shallow cave and then moved a giant stone to seal the front of it. He was placed where no human hand could ever touch him again. His journey was now complete. His body was at rest, and his spirit was at one with his Designer.

Abel was home.

CHAPTER 18

Abel lived ...

Had a seed gone back into the ground? Was this what Wisdom was talking about?

I sat for a long time in a tree outside the cave. The Designer had allowed me to linger here. Many thoughts were running through my mind. I began replaying the events of the day, but each of them kept ending up as questions. Wisdom had left when the Designer walked back through Eden, so I was here alone.

I wanted to understand all that had happened. I wanted to sit with Miriam, with Eve, and then with Adam. A part of me had also wanted to sit where they had sat, by Abel's bloodied body, to allow my talons to dig deeper into the ground. So great was this pain, though, that I wondered if I could go deep enough through it to reach His love again. Were some pains just too big to be healed? Would their grief ever disappear?

As I sat, the words of Abel came back to me, "Eagle, you have been tasked to watch over all things. It is a wonderful task you have been given. But, Eagle, can you see all things?" This phrase kept me here. I was no longer here to watch; I wanted to see. Something had shifted within me that day.

As the Designer walked away from the cave, a sensation happened within me. While the Designer was there, I felt life. Not just His life, but also Abel's. Now that he had been gone for many hours, I could no longer feel Abel's life. I quickly understood that a body is a place to house a person's spirit. The body is fragile and needs constant care for it to be maintained, but the spirit is different; it requires a different source of nourishment. I think I was beginning to see.

My mind was racing now, and I could feel some of the mystery becoming clearer. I think I was beginning to grasp the reason we live at all. We live to love, and this is surely the nourishment that sustains and grows the spirit. How could I have missed that? The Designer hid this fact in plain sight. Every time He came near me, I wanted to soar. I wanted to laugh. I wanted to … love …

Suddenly, I felt Abel's presence again, and it was as if I heard his voice, "Eagle, you are no longer watching; you are seeing."

It was so real I immediately thought the body had returned to life and was speaking to me. It felt as if Abel was speaking to me. I was hearing Abel's voice in my head. It was then I realized the Designer must be near me. I spun around to see Him watching me. The smile on His face told me I had thought correctly. I was now seeing!

He said to me, "Well done, my good and faithful servant. I have given you the privilege of understanding the mysteries of my Kingdom. Eagle, from this day forward, I will no longer call you my servant; you will be forever known as my friend."

My heart was racing to hear these words. My natural impulse was to take flight and soar into the sky, for today was no ordinary day; today was the day I began to see.

"My Lord, I will forever cling to these words. You honor me far beyond what I feel I deserve. Please thank Abel for me. He opened my eyes to see."

The Designer smiled and nodded and said, "He knows."

What followed was silence, and I could see He was thinking, so I waited. It was always worth the wait.

"Beyond what you feel you deserve? What an interesting statement, Eagle." He paused and said, "A child does not earn a parent's love, nor does it ask if they deserve the parent's love. The child is simply loved. It is not deserving nor undeserving of that love. It is the same with you. Let us not talk about deserving or undeserving of my love. I simply love you."

Then He continued, "Do you love me, Eagle?"

He so loved to ask me this question, and I always loved to respond to it.

"Yes, my Lord, I do love you," I responded. The Designer loved to be loved as much as He loved me.

"Can I ask a question, my Lord?"

"Yes, Eagle, ask anything you like," he replied.

"Long ago, Wisdom spoke to me about a seed that needed to be sown into the ground for new life to come. Is this what I witnessed today when you laid Abel's body in the cave?"

"Eagle, Wisdom spoke to you of another who will be laid into a cave much like this, but many more years must pass before this event happens. When it does, you will not need to ask if it has or hasn't happened; you will know. This is another event that you will not merely watch, but you will see. What you have witnessed today is a foretaste of what is to come."

"Come now, Eagle, we have much to do, and soon the sun will rise."

CHAPTER 19

"We need to visit Adam and Eve, for they need to be the first to hear what I am about to do," the Designer said.

At that, we set off. The last thing I wanted to do was leave Eden, and I wanted to linger longer, but really, even if I did, I would still long for more time there. This is the time of day that I love the most, and when I was living here, I would spread my wings to soar over it all and do what I had been commissioned to do: to watch. Oh, how that word has now transformed me. Never again will I be simply 'watching.' Now, I have the ability to see.

I was watching the Designer move through Eden below me. Most days, when I followed Him, I would have plenty of time to soar, as He would rarely move fast. But, today, He was moving swiftly. Before long, He was walking past *the two trees* in the middle of Eden. Seeing those *two trees* now triggers so many beautiful memories of being there. A pang of sorrow went through my whole body, though, for, at the same time as there were good memories, there was always that memory when everything seemed to unravel.

It is an odd memory for me to unravel. I will never forget Adam and Eve, wearing as many leaves as they could sew together, and there was also the strange mocking lizard. At the same time, Wisdom had sat next to me in a tree which I could now see had grown much since the day we sat there. It was there Wisdom told me of the great love story beginning to unfold. She spoke to me of hope, not hopelessness. She told me of the Designer's great plan and that none of this surprised him. It was so hard to understand back then, but all these years later, I was seeing the beginnings of His great plan. I was no longer watching; I was seeing. I'm not sure I'll ever tire of reminding myself of this one thing.

By the time I realized I had been circling *the two trees,* the Designer was no longer in the clearing. He was nearly across the river. So I took one more look at the great *Tree of Life.* It was the largest one in Eden. I then remembered back to when I was first created and the first time I saw that *tree.* It was smaller then, but even so, it was still magnificent. Its fruit was like no other fruit I had seen. It contained all the colors of creation. One could be mesmerized by gazing into it. And the taste ... it would be impossible for me to describe, for its taste would change. That might sound odd, but it is true. When you bite an apple, you don't need to open your eyes to know that you have bitten an apple. It tastes, feels, and smells like an apple. This fruit, though, was different. The taste would depend on what you were going through at the time. If you were joy-filled, then somehow the fruit tasted like joy. If you were peace-filled and content, then the taste was something that soothed your soul. If you were feeling lonely, then there was something in it that drew you to love. It's hard to explain, but I can only say that if you ever get a chance to eat it, you will not be disappointed. In fact, you will heal.

The Designer was now halfway to Adam and Eve's home. Even from a distance, I could see the atmosphere there was different from what I had just experienced. The closer I flew to their home, the more I could sense the grief overflowing it. I needed to remind myself that they had not seen what I had just seen. Their last image of Abel was bloodsoaked and lifeless ...

On the way there, I flew over the area where Abel had died. It was such an odd feeling to look again upon a place where the greatest destruction I had witnessed had occurred. Something about it, though, drew me to the ground. I was ahead of the Designer now, and I knew I had time before He got to Adam's place, so I landed beside the blood-soaked ground. Yesterday I was scared to put my talons into the ground for fear of the pain that I would feel. That was yesterday, though, and much had changed for me. So I sunk my talons into the very earth that held the blood of Abel. The pain was searing as I did. It blazed through every part of my body. I had never felt such pain before. Everything within me screamed to let go and fly away, but I knew healing would come to me if I sought the love that flowed through all things.

I closed my eyes and allowed the pain to move through my body. I could feel the grief of many hearts, but then I felt something I did not expect to feel ... I felt remorse. It was beyond the pain, and yet it was like a new pain. There was such sadness in what I felt, even despair. Where was this feeling coming from?

As if answering my thoughts and surprising me at the same time, the Designer seated beside me said, "You are feeling Cain, Eagle. He is lost, and we need to find him. His anger has now subsided, and he despairs because this is a problem he cannot fix. Every other problem he encountered, he was able to fix with the strength of his arm and the knowledge he had gained. He has learned today that there are some problems strength and knowledge cannot fix."

I looked up from the ground and realized I was seeing the final images Abel's eyes would have seen. Off in the distance were the sheep that he had named and loved. Beyond that, there were the mountains that he loved to walk through. There were times when

I saw him and Miriam walking amongst the trees and adventuring beyond where they had been before. Miriam always asked him questions about Eden; its trees and its flowers fascinated her. Abel was always willing to listen to each and every question. To answer them, he would often lead her to a tree similar to the one she asked about or a flower with the same scent. He took so much time to help her understand and experience what she was asking about. She discovered much about the Designer through the moments she spent wandering with Abel.

Even as I sit here with the Designer, I can remember a time when Abel and Miriam sat on that distant mountain. It's the tallest one I can see from here, and it took them three days to get to the top of it. Abel always wanted to see more of the Designer's work, and, like Cain, he would go where few others would venture. Miriam loved being with him; if he was climbing a high mountain, she would climb it as well.

That day as I was 'watching' them on the mountain ... it made me laugh to myself about using that word now, but that was my task ... I was soaring high above. The thermal winds were exhilarating to find and soar higher, and they were usually found near the mountains. One side of the mountain was a sheer cliff face, and when the wind would hit it just right ... well ... let's say there was hardly a greater feeling than allowing it to take me higher than I had been before.

I had been following them for days as they climbed. I could see Abel explaining something to Miriam at every stop they made. After three more days of hiking, they made it to the summit, and waiting there for them was the Designer. He'd been there all along. In the evenings, I had gone to sit and talk with Him. Then there were times I did not need a reason other than to feel the love that flowed through Him.

As they arrived, Miriam was obviously surprised to find Him there and must have wondered how He had overtaken them. Abel, though, just smiled. The Designer had done this many times to him, and it was like a game that He played with Abel—the shock Abel used to have had long been replaced with expectancy. I could sense Abel's growing excitement as he neared the top of the mountain that day.

Abel and Miriam turned to look in every direction, awed by all they could see. The eyes the Designer had given me could see much further than theirs, but even the view they could see was stunning. They stood in silence for many minutes as they rotated around and around to see all of what was in front of them. Their home was so far away they could no longer make out the people, but they could barely make out the smoke that rose from the fires cooking the lunchtime meals.

The Designer and I sat, experiencing the joy that flowed from both of their spirits. Their awe and joy were combining. This became another one of those extraordinary moments when I saw the glow in Abel and, this time, also in Miriam. To be there to witness this was precious to me, and I felt it was a gift that was beautiful beyond words. I do not know if I ever saw Miriam so happy. Then soon, as it often did, her joy turned to a song. I loved it when Miriam would sing. She had pieced together each song, and they came straight from her spirit. She had a voice that would shift the atmosphere surrounding her. Celebration and love were in every melody and note of her voice.

She sang words of praise for the Designer. She sang words of love for Abel. She sang words that testified of her journey; that day, she sang words of her future. She spoke of the wonders that would come and the love that would bind a family together. As she sang, I watched the Designer, and He became lost in His thoughts and her voice. It was as if He was transported to another time, a time where there was no shame, and He was doing what He loved to do ... create.

Later I asked the Designer about this, and He said, "Each person I created in my image, every single one. They each carry something unique about me, and no one else carries what Miriam carries. Today we have both experienced the flow of her unique design. Did you feel the love in her voice, Eagle?"

"Yes, my Lord, but I also felt something more. There was a deeper cry within her. It was like a desire she has but is not yet fulfilled. Did you feel that, my Lord?"

"Yes, I did. She desires to give Abel a child, but so far, she has had no child to give him. Her heart is sad, and often when she talks with me, she asks for this desire to be fulfilled."

As I recalled that memory, I came crashing back into the present and realized that this desire would never be met, and I simply wept. More questions were rising in my spirit, but I did not have the words to form them ... so great was the grief that I felt at that moment. My tears were added to the ground, just like Miriam's had last night. This one moment in time had caused so much sorrow and pain.

The Designer still sat beside me, and to my surprise, His hands also were in the ground. His eyes were closed, and tears were also falling from His eyes. He, too, was enduring the pain ... He was bringing healing to the land ... was this the seed? I wondered to myself.

After a long time, the Designer lifted His head and said, "Eagle, you have another question."

He always seemed to know, or maybe He just knew I was always curious.

"Yes, my Lord, I do, but I feel too sad even to mention it ..." He waited for me, like He always would, until finally, I blurted out, "Miriam wanted Abel's child, and now she cannot."

The Designer smiled, looked into my eyes, and said, "Do you remember the time up on that distant mountain?" I nodded through my tears. "Do you remember the song that she sang?"

Again, I nodded through more tears, and remembering it again brought a fresh wave of grief to me. "Do you remember what I told you, Eagle? I said to you, 'She desires to give Abel a child, but so far, she has had no child to give him.' Do you remember this, Eagle?"

"Yes, my Lord, I remember it like it was yesterday," I said.

"But so far," He repeated himself.

"Yes, my Lord, forgive me, but what does 'but so far' mean? Will she partner with another man again and have children with him? Will this be giving her the desire of her heart when she dearly wanted to have a child with Abel?" The tears still flowed. I had never talked this way to the Designer, and a part of me felt I was wrong to say this, so I said, "I am sorry, my Lord, I should not have spoken like that to you. You know far more than me. I will be quiet now."

He responded, "Should? Who told you that word?"

This shocked me, it was the same conversation I had with Wisdom, and she told me it is a word that friends do not use. What was the Designer saying? What did He mean when He said, 'But so far?' I looked to Him but found it difficult to look into His eyes. I did not want to repeat the wrong thing, and I still felt shame at speaking to Him as I had.

The Designer put his hand under my chin and lifted it, so the only way I could not look into His eyes was to close my own. The tears were still flowing, and it was a fight just to open my eyes.

Then he said, "Eagle, friends do not use the word 'should'. I have called you my friend, and my friend you are. You are free to say anything you like to me, and friends are able to speak the truth to each other because of the love that we have shared."

He then continued, "You wonder about the phrase I use, as if it is a metaphor, but it is not. 'But so far' means she had yet to have Abel's child." There was a long pause, and then he softly said, "Eagle, she carries Abel's child."

I was so stunned that I staggered backward, releasing my talons from the ground. Words came flooding out of my mouth, "Does she know? Did Abel know? Did anyone know?"

"Yes, Eagle, that day on the mountain. Do you remember when I sat with them and asked you to take flight and soar? You were disappointed at the time because you wanted to stay with the three of us. What I had to tell them was for their ears alone. I shared with them that the desire of their hearts would be fulfilled. I also spoke to them about Cain and the anger that he harbored."

"Did you tell them that Cain would kill Abel?" I could not help the words that tumbled from me. Somewhere between my curiosity and my grief, I could not hold them back. Then, everything slowed down again as I realized what I had said, "Did you know Cain would kill Abel? Could you have stopped this from happening? Could you have prevented the pain so many are experiencing?"

The Designer waited until all of my questions had run out. There was a long silence that followed. I then realized that my questions had become accusations, and I had not intended them to be so; I just did not understand what was happening. I felt that I had gone back to watching and was no longer seeing.

He was always so patient with me. After a while, He stirred, cleared His voice, and said, "Eagle, I could have done all you said." There was such grief in His words. I was sorry that I'd even asked the questions at all, and I hated seeing Him sad.

"Your questions need to be asked, and they require an answer. In the generations ahead, many people will ask me the same questions. If you are willing to listen, I will give you the knowledge you seek. It will be up to you then to let that knowledge become understanding."

While this was confusing to me at the moment, I wanted to hear His voice and listen to His words more than anything else. They brought me life every time He spoke, and today I wanted to feel that life again.

"Eagle, place your talons into the ground again. Like before, go beyond the pain and the remorse, and ground yourself in my love."

This action was now something I was becoming familiar with. The pain no longer frightened me, for I knew the love that awaited me. So, I let my talons sink beneath the surface. There was the familiar pain, and then there was the grief. Again, I felt Cain's remorse and even Adam and Eve's loss. Deeper still was His love; to feel it was to receive healing and life simultaneously.

The Designer then continued, "Eagle, to have prevented this awful moment from occurring, I would have needed to take from Cain his choice. In taking his choice, I would have stopped loving him. What I need to do now with Cain will require my love, not my indifference and nor my anger. If I stop loving him, I will have no mercy for him."

There was silence for a while, and I was happy it was so. What I was hearing was overwhelming, unraveling me and teaching me simultaneously. His love is not simply an expression of who He is; it is who He is. He was revealing His design to me. It is something I have known and been taught before, but now, it was a deeper revelation of His love.

When He spoke again, He said, "To remove love, even in this time, would remove me from Cain. Like Adam, Eve, Miriam, and even you, Cain needs me to be true to who I am."

Once again, my mind raced. Somehow, I knew in my heart everything the Designer was speaking was right, but at the same time, I wanted Cain to be punished for what he had done. Cain needed to be accountable.

The Designer, again, knew my thoughts. "Eagle, Cain will receive the consequences for what he has done, and whether I do it or the family does it, it matters not. Right now, his own heart has made him accountable. He knows he cannot fix this, and he knows he has broken every bond of love by this act. The remorse you feel is his remorse, and it is real. But I will not repay death with death. You are about to see something no one has seen. You will witness death being repaid with life."

I sat and replayed the words the Designer said to me. He said, 'It will be up to you to let that knowledge become understanding.' It then dawned on me, my knowledge up until this moment demanded a ledger be balanced. My knowledge demanded that if a life is taken, then another will be taken to balance it. For knowledge to become understanding, though ... what did that mean? I slowly thought through this until the revelation rolled over me like a wave on the ocean. The Designer did not speak in terms of ledgers or balances. He always spoke in terms of love. This knowledge needed to be heard through His love and not through my judgment. My knowledge demanded that death was the cost of death. If that were true, everything is in ruin, and there could be no life.

The Designer simply smiled and, leaning over to me, said, "The watchman is now the see-er."

"Come now, again; we still need to go to Adam and Eve."

CHAPTER 20

It didn't take us long to get there. We were greeted by a silent family. No one looked like they knew what to say or do. Some had cooked meals, but it seemed nobody was hungry. Some had left flowers in an attempt to bring some level of life to their door.

As the Designer got close to the door, Eve came out to meet Him. It was apparent she had cried most of the night and had not slept. She seemed not to care who saw her like this, but at least she welcomed the Designer. He held her in His arms for a long time; He was in no rush, and she needed to feel the love He carried.

The Designer eventually said, "Eve, where is Adam?"

She replied, "My Lord, I do not know. After we came home, he said he felt numb and wanted to be alone. He could not be alone with so many people visiting to bring food. I think he just went to find some quiet place to mourn."

The Designer simply held her. Once Adam returned, He would tell them both all that had happened to Abel. But, for now, Eve needed His comfort. This was not the first time the Designer had comforted her, either. Few know it, but before Adam and Eve left

Eden, the Designer went to her and held her like He was holding her now. Back then, there were very few words as well; her sorrow and grief needed to feel His comfort.

Eve eventually invited us to sit around her fire and wait for Adam. The Designer had every intention of staying there and made himself comfortable. Eve brought Him a warm spiced drink that smelled like it contained honey. He motioned for me to come over, and in a voice only I could hear, he said, "Go and find Adam. See if he is willing to come home. Tell him the Designer needs to see him."

At that, I took flight. My leaving did not seem to bother Eve, and I doubt anything could have upset her tired and grieving spirit. She needed to sleep, but her grief would not let her body relax. The embrace of the Designer had helped, and at least, by the time I left, she was beginning to talk.

There were many times I flew over this family. Adam was always somewhere close to home. He loved his home. But today, he was nowhere to be found. I widened my circle of flight, and each completed circle would take me out further and further again, but I could not find him.

Something then made me think of the digging tool that had killed Abel. I had seen Adam toss it away from the scene, hoping Eve would not have seen it. I flew back to the place of Abel's death and to the area the tool had been thrown, and neither Adam nor the tool was there.

There was another place I had not looked yet, and a big part of me did not want to go there ... Cain's workshop ... I did not know if Adam would be there or not, but I decided I should at least look. When I got there, I heard the same noises coming out of the workshop as the night when Cain's anger had been released. Surely Cain had not returned here. I waited for a while, hoping whoever it was would come out. When that didn't happen, I flew to a window, and to my surprise, it wasn't Cain in the workshop, it was Adam, and he was furious.

I had never witnessed Adam this angry. He was usually subdued and hated making a scene; this was so unlike him. He obviously did not care who heard what he was doing, and this was so out of character for him.

He was always happy when his boys got attention. He was so proud of them. He would often tell me of Cain's mighty harvest or how he bent the mighty Euphrates River to irrigate the land, allowing wider fields to grow crops. And he would speak just as highly of Abel. He was so proud of Abel showing how a sheep's wool could be used for clothing without harming the sheep.

Today, though, was a different day. Adam's family had been torn in half by the wielder of the digging tool. I flew back to the same tree I had waited for Cain. This time, I waited for Adam.

I was sure that, by now, word had gone out about Abel's death and Cain's absence. Most knew they were not as close as they once had been, but for Cain to be totally absent with no one knowing where he was … things would not have been adding up. People seem to have a way of creating their own narratives when there is an absence of facts. So who knows what has been spoken by all the people?

Eventually, the noise inside subsided. As it did, I noticed another voice in there. Amongst the things being thrown and angry words being spoken to the walls, I could hear Adam talking to someone. Who was he speaking to? I knew if I flew over and landed on the roof this time, the sound of it all would be clearly heard in the workshop. I wanted Adam to know I was here. As I landed on the roof, I heard the two voices go quiet beneath me. A short while later, Adam came out to investigate and found me.

"Adam," I said, "Who are you talking to?"

"No one," he retorted back to me.

"At first, I thought you were yelling at the walls, but then I heard another voice. It was a voice I was familiar with, but I was having trouble placing it. Who were you talking to?"

Adam had not said another word when, from the corner of my eye, I saw the snake that was coiled up beside Cain. It was trying to slither away from the workshop with no one noticing. I watched it go off into the bushes. As it left, a peculiar thing happened to Adam. It was like he had awoken from some kind of dream. He literally shook himself awake, and before I knew it, I could once again see the sadness in his eyes. What had that snake said to him?

"Adam," I said, "The Designer wishes to see you. He is waiting at your home with Eve, and He asks you to come straight away."

"Eagle, I have nothing to say to Him today. Everything has been lost. One boy lies dead, and another has fled. What could He possibly have to say to me?"

"Sometimes, Adam, it's not about the words He speaks; it is about the presence He carries," I said. "You know the presence I speak of; I know you have experienced it."

"I have, Eagle, that is true. But I have never lost so much. For you to be here at Cain's workshop, you must suspect what I believe to be true of Abel's death. Cain's digging tool was found near his brother's body ... Who else could have done it? Everyone loved Abel ... everyone except Cain. For years, Eagle, I could feel and see His jealousy toward Abel, and I put it down to a brotherly quarrel that would soon be soothed. I should have been there for them. I should have been a better father; I should have done more."

There was that word again, 'should'. Now was not the time to give Adam the same lesson that Wisdom and the Designer had given me about using that word. I could hear the pained cry of regret in that word and the desire of Adam's heart to be a better father. It was too late, and Adam knew it. Adam would not get to have that conversation with Abel until he, himself, was laid into the dirt like Abel was.

"Adam, the Designer has answers to your questions; I do not. He knows how to comfort you in ways I cannot. What I know is … you are a good man, and you have loved your sons as well as you could have. Now, please come and allow the Designer to soothe your anger, hurt, and the pain you carry. You were not designed to carry this alone."

Reluctantly, Adam walked away from the workshop and in the direction of his home. He seemed uplifted a little by knowing the Designer was at his home. I know how much he loved spending time with Him. I, though, stayed a while longer. That snake had again caught my attention, and it needed to be dealt with.

Snakes don't usually come out on cold nights. However, I wasn't dealing with a normal snake; this one seemed to love the darkness, so I waited. It was not long after Adam had left that I noticed movement again in the bushes, and it was only a slight movement, and most animals wouldn't have even noticed it.

One of the wonders of my wingspan is I can take flight silently, and being such a dark night; I would not even cast a shadow. The snake would not see me coming. With one more movement in the bushes, I would pinpoint my target. It did not see me coming and didn't know what hit it. I grabbed the snake right behind its head. It tried in vain to strike at me, and my hold on the snake only got tighter each time it did. Initially, it hissed at me, but when it realized hissing did nothing to me, it spoke … and there was that same familiar voice I had heard at the foot of *The Tree of Knowledge of Good and Bad* … the voice of the strange lizard.

It screamed at me, "Let me go. You have no right to be holding me like this. Even if you kill me, you now know I can come back and possess another."

"Oh, I'm not going to kill you, snake. I'm going to take you to the Designer. If there is one thing I have learned from Him, it is this: when my mercy ceases, a little piece of my spirit dies. So it is not death I bring you, but mercy."

The rest of the flight to Adam's home, there were no verbal threats to me or to those I loved. The closer I got to the Designer, though, the more frantic the snake became. Its day of reckoning had come.

CHAPTER 21

"Eagle, what have you brought me?" the Designer asked.

I had landed and dropped the talking snake at His feet, and He was not scared of it at all. Eve and Miriam were nowhere to be seen; it was just the Designer and me.

"My Lord, this is the talking snake I saw coiled up beside Cain when he was on his way to bring you his gift. Today, I found it again at Cain's house. It is also where I found Adam. It tried to slither away when Adam came out from Cain's workshop. Initially, Adam was angry with me and refused to come, but he calmed down after the snake had slithered away. I did not want to let it escape, so I waited there until it tried to come back into the workshop."

"Why did you not kill it, Eagle?" the Designer asked me.

"Because of you, my Lord."

The Designer smiled at that and said, "Now, Eagle, what do you want me to do with it?"

"It is not natural for this snake to distort your creation or your design, and I have witnessed this hideous voice corrupt your design more than once. I also know that all of your creation is good, so there is goodness in this snake, and I just cannot see it yet."

"Eagle, you have seen much this day, and in this, you have discovered a great truth. The snake is not your enemy."

The snake was backed up into a corner from which it could not escape; it was afraid. Here it was behaving completely the opposite from before. It was trying to get as far from the Designer as it could. Whatever was happening here, something within it was at work. It had no fear of me, but it feared for its life in front of the Designer.

"My Lord, why is the snake so scared of you?" I asked.

"It fears where I can send it," He replied.

This intrigued me, "Where can you send it, My Lord?"

The Designer turned back to the snake and asked it, "Where did you come from?"

The snake appeared to be groveling now, "From my master."

"And what were your master's orders?" He asked.

"To sow doubt," it replied.

The Designer turned back to me and said, "Eagle, there are more things happening here than even your magnificent eyes can see. If you are willing to see, I will show you more."

"I am willing, my Lord," I responded.

"Eagle, do you remember when we were in Eden, and you saw the glow within Abel?"

"Yes, it was only yesterday, but I will never forget it, my Lord," I replied.

"You saw Abel's spirit. It is alive, it is eternal, and now it is within me, but you can no longer see it. He is in a realm that is difficult to see, but it can be easily felt. I think you know of what I speak. You testified to it when you felt the change in Adam when the snake left him. He was angry, but once it left his presence, he calmed down. It will now be the same when we eventually speak to Cain. The voice in this snake is of the realm that I speak of.

It has possessed the snake's spirit and has changed the snake's character. Today I will release the snake of this unwelcome visitor and send it back to the realm it came from."

This was all new to me. I had indeed felt the things that the Designer spoke of, and I could testify to it so clearly that I began to understand what He was saying.

The Designer turned back to the snake and said, "How many of you are sowing seeds of doubt in my creation?"

"We are many," whispered the snake. "Legions of corrupted ones have been sent across your creation to corrupt all that has been created." The snake's voice grew in boldness as it continued, "There are more of us than these people can see, and many more of the ones that have been created in your image will fall because of us." The voice in the snake was now defiant.

The Designer, however, was not troubled at all by the voice. He simply turned back to me and said, "What it is saying is true. Many of these voices were once my friends. I had made them before I made Adam and Eve. I gave them the ability to choose, just as I have given this to all I have created. Some of them used that ability to supplant and harm, and this is one of them."

"So why not destroy them all?" I exclaimed. "If this is their purpose, then why are they allowed to live?"

"Here is a knowledge that is hard for many to understand," He said. "Eagle, I am life. Everything that lives gains its life through me, even the voice inside the snake. To kill it would take some of my life. That day may come, but today is not a day for death to have its final say. Today is a day for life to abound."

Yes, truly, this was a hard thing to understand. How could these realms exist? Surely they would always be at war with each other. I was confused, and the Designer could see it in me. I could see He was waiting for me to ask a question, but what was there to ask? So what came tumbling out of my mouth was, "I just don't understand."

"Few do, Eagle," He replied, "Few do."

I could sense loneliness in the Designer as these words seemed to drift out of Him. I wanted to be one of the 'few' He was talking about. My mind was wrestling to find the right solution here, but everything I thought seemed to end in me asking the Designer to break His own design.

Finally, He said, "To answer the questions you are asking, imagine this: Go back to Eden in your imagination."

This was becoming easier for me to do, especially with all the practice I have had lately. I desperately wanted to be back there and see Abel eat from *The Tree of Life*!

"Once you are there, ask your questions again, but choose which *tree* you will sit under to ask them."

The Designer waited for me to settle before He continued, "Eagle, which *tree* are you sitting under to gain your answers? Are you only interested in what is right and wrong, or are you looking for life?"

Immediately I understood what He was saying, but at the same time, I did not. As soon as I pictured those *two trees* in my imagination, I could clearly see myself under *The Tree of Knowledge of Good and Bad*. I was only looking for a 'Good' outcome and attempting to do everything that would prevent a 'Bad' one.

The Designer was reading my thoughts again, and He was smiling at me. "Now that you have understood what is 'Good' and 'Bad', and you can see where they lead you, what would 'Life' look like?"

This was a hard question for me, for to fix this situation, I believed death needed to be dealt out to those who brought death into the world. However, for the Designer to bring death would contradict His very nature and break down His own design. If His design broke down … what would that mean for all I see and love?

"Eagle, in the days to come, many will use my name and appear to speak as if they have spent time directly with me. Here is the way to test if they have. You will know them by their love, not by the strength of their voice. You will also recognize which *tree* in Eden they are positioned under. If you only hear 'Good' and 'Bad', or 'right' and 'wrong', that will be the fruit they are feasting on. If you encounter 'Life' coming from them, then that is the fruit they are feasting on."

The Designer always likes to speak in metaphors. But, under the actual *Tree of Life*, I had discovered healing from my shame. But now, in my imagination, I was clearly seeing what He was speaking of. It was a lesson I would never forget and one that would continue to ground me in understanding His design and His heart.

"So, my Lord, what will you do with the snake?" I asked.

"I will free the snake and banish the spirit from my presence," He replied.

At that, he turned again to the snake and picked it up from the corner it had been trapped in. The voice trapped inside the snake was whimpering; it obviously feared being cast out of His presence. To the snake, He simply whispered, "Let go of this spirit; it is not part of your design."

I was transfixed by what I was seeing. The snake visibly relaxed in the Designer's hand and fell straight into a deep sleep. In the process of relaxing, the voice yelped and then was silent. The Designer then addressed the speaker of the voice as if He could clearly see it, "Go back to your master and tell him his mission has failed again."

At that, the Designer placed the snake in a nearby tree and then returned to warm His hands by the fire. We sat for hours talking about all I had seen. Soon it would be the time of day He loved the most, the cool of the evening. He looked up and past me and said, "Adam is arriving, and it is time we welcomed him home."

CHAPTER 22

As the evil one fled from His presence, the Designer rose to meet Adam. Eve, too, had been awaiting this moment. She burst from the house as soon as she heard the Designer greet him. Ever since the time in Eden when the strange lizard had separated them, she did not enjoy being alone.

Seeing them meet was both precious and heart-wrenching. The bond between them could be felt; they dearly loved each other—this past day, though, had stretched them both to the breaking point. Adam had disappeared and left Eve to deal with the mourners, the meals, the flowers, and Miriam.

"Where have you been?" I heard her whisper to him. There are moments when I hear multiple emotions in one phrase; this was one of them. I could feel her sadness, frustration, and loneliness come tumbling from her.

Adam could see the Designer waiting behind Eve, and instead of answering, he used the Designer to avoid her question. I could be wrong, but I felt Eve was hurt by his avoidance.

I do not think it was lost on the Designer, either.

"Come here and sit by the fire. Let us talk like we used to in Eden at this time," He said to them both.

After they settled by the fire, the Designer looked straight into Adam's eyes and said, "Eve asked where you have been. Maybe we could start by you answering her question."

Adam dropped his head; he looked utterly defeated. It was a question that could unravel so much. Would he tell Eve of his destructive rampage at Cain's workshop? Would he tell her of the digging tool he hid at the site of Abel's death? Would he share his conversation with the talking snake? Would he say that he had been called here by the Designer and not by his desire to be with her?

"What does it matter where I was? Our son is dead."

Adam's voice trailed off as he spoke. Was this the first time he had said it out loud? Was he confirming the ugly truth by saying it? It seemed he wanted to shift the attention.

He turned to the Designer and said, "Our son would not have been dead if you had been there." Then gaining strength, he continued, "You told us that family would be hard when we left Eden. This is not 'hard'; this is impossible."

The Designer responded gently, "Loss of this kind is irreparable." After a few moments, He continued, "It is irreparable, but it can be healed."

Adam exclaimed, "Now you are speaking in riddles again. Speak plainly. Tell us what you mean."

Adam's anger had spilled from him, but it still felt like a distraction from what was happening deep within him. He had known healing before. He had dug his fingers into the ground, both in Eden and here in this land; he knew the love of the Designer. But, here, he was lost in his grief. The Designer did not react to Adam's anger; He simply allowed Adam to express it. I wished the Designer had taken Adam and Eve back to *The Tree of Life* with Abel's body and let them see what I saw. The Designer would have a reason why he did not take them with us, but now was not the time to ask; now was a time to heal.

The Designer then said, "You have run away, Adam. When Eve needed you the most, you ran away. You know who did this awful act, and yet you have chosen to hide it from her. I had to send Eagle to go and find you, and he found you talking to a snake."

None of this was spoken harshly, as the Designer would never have spoken heartlessly to Adam. Each word that came from His mouth felt like it had been soaked with His love. He is literally the definition of love, and the language He spoke was love. This was the very force that made creation happen. And now, in this moment, this creation force of love combined with the truth became an invitation to be free.

Adam broke down and wept. He knew it was all true, but he did not know how to put words around it. To his left, I could see Eve bristle when the Designer spoke of the talking snake. There were still wounds from her first encounter with that strange lizard that would cause her to react physically when someone would talk about it, but having Adam confess to speaking to another one ...

Eve challenged him, "Adam, please tell me this isn't true. Tell me that Eagle lied. Tell me why you were at Cain's workshop."

Her challenges became less as the realization of what the Designer had said started to sink in ... 'you know who did this awful act' ... I am certain she had already thought of who it could have been, but saying it aloud must have been a far harder thing to do.

After a long silence, Adam said, "Eagle did not lie."

His admission was met with a wail that came from the depths of Eve, "No, no, no, no, no," she kept repeating. There was nothing anyone could do at this moment. Eve was dealing with the most heartbreaking news a mother could receive. I could see her breathing speed up, and I grew concerned that she would feint right before us. The shock was too much for one person to bear.

Adam stepped towards her to hold her, but as he held her, she started beating his chest, and all she would say was, "No."

Time stood still at that moment. We all knew that there were no words to soothe her spirit. As with Adam, she needed to express her pain and grief, and we needed to let her. So we waited. How long we waited, I could not tell. To love Eve well, we needed to wait.

Suddenly, Eve broke from Adam's grip and demanded, "Did you see Cain? Did he say that he did it?"

Adam shook his head at both questions. It was like he would not dare utter another word because of the pain his words had caused her. When Eve saw his denial, she became defiant, "If you have not seen him and he has not confessed to this, then how do you know he did it? Maybe he is off on one of his adventures out past the mountains and was not here at all."

Adam simply shrugged his shoulders and opened his hands in a gesture he had nothing more to say. He knew what he knew and could not see another outcome as to who killed Abel. He had these same thoughts before he went to Cain's workshop, but after seeing it in disarray and meeting the talking snake there, all doubt disappeared. Then we watched as his anger reappeared. Instead of yelling at the Designer, he rose and walked a distance away and yelled at the sky. I could not tell what he yelled, but every part of his body combined to express his anger and grief.

When he returned, we could see the exhaustion on his face; he looked like he had aged a hundred years in a day. It was obvious Adam knew he needed to tell Eve everything now.

Then, in a voice that could not hide his broken heart, he said, "Eve, my heart and my love, I found Cain's digging tool beside Abel yesterday. When I saw it, I hid it. I could not believe or cope with knowing Cain had done this. Yes, it is true someone else could have used his tool, so I went to his workshop to find him. He was not there, but the place was a mess. You know Cain would never treat his tools like that. The tools he used daily were no longer there, and his digging tool was missing too. I then looked for his extra clothes, and they were gone too. It was then I discovered the talking snake. I wish I had never talked with it," spitting these words out as he said them. "It laughed at me and mocked me. It told me how our son died. Then it told me we would never see Cain again, either. He told me it was all the Designer's fault and doing. I was so easily deceived. Forgive me, my love."

With that last word, Adam's voice trailed off and was met with Eve in full fury, "You listened to that thing? Surely you know it is lying. Adam, we have been here before. It is not telling the truth. It is entirely evil!"

Adam whispered his response, "I know, my love, I know."

Eve then turned her fury on the Designer, "Is this true?" she demanded from Him.

At that, the Designer moved to Eve and placed His arms around her again. Like with Adam, she pounded His chest and let her anger be made known to anyone within hearing distance. I could see a crowd forming; the noise and yelling had drawn them out of their homes and away from their meals.

Eve was angry, but she was also tired beyond comprehension. Soon, the strength of her blows became less and less. When they had ceased, the Designer leaned down and whispered into her ear, "Eve, your son, Cain, still lives. In that, the snake lied to Adam." He allowed His words to settle in her understanding before He continued. "But it is true this terrible moment happened by his hands. He knows what he has done, and he is filled with despair and regret. I will go to him and show him my love and my mercy. You have felt my love and mercy before, Eve. Today, Cain also needs to feel this."

Eve's tears continued to flow. So much had changed for her.

The Designer gently continued, "Abel's death cannot be reversed. Much like what happened to you all in Eden, choices were made that cannot be unmade. As I have said, the choices made are irreparable, but they can be healed. You need to trust me, Eve."

Eve just continued to sob. Adam was standing apart from them, and I could see his despair and grief overwhelming his mind and body; he did not know what to do.

The Designer lifted Eve's tear-stained face and said, "Eve, do you love me?"

Eve replied, "Yes, my Lord, I do love you, but right now, my heart is torn. I want to know why, and yet, my heart breaks for my Cain as well."

When she continued, her despair became pleading, "Lord, I have lost both my sons, yet one still lives. I long to see him again. I do not know what I would do if I saw him again, but I want to hold my son, the only one I have left. Please, my Lord, make him come home to me. I have nothing more to lose; I have lost everything."

It looked like Adam had nothing left to lose as well. His anger was now spent. He was tired and heartbroken. He looked numb and lost in his thoughts as Eve continued to plead with the Designer.

Eve's tears then replaced all the words she could have spoken; they took on a language of pain and suffering of their own. How much their lives had changed in the past two days. From proud parents with two sons who had been flourishing in this land, to this ... It seemed the Designer had been wrong for a short while as family had not been difficult, and the land was productive. But now, everything has changed.

As Eve soaked the Designer's clothing with her tears, He softly said, "Eve, I cannot make Cain come to you. I know your great pain; I feel it too. But to make him do anything against his will would be to take away his power to choose. You both know I will not remove this from him or anyone. No, Eve, I will not do that."

Another wave of raw grief and tears flowed from Eve. Her sobbing cry was felt by the growing crowd that was building around them. Nobody knew what to say ... But really, what was there to say?

"Right now, Cain needs my mercy; he does not need my control."

Eve simply nodded, and Adam dropped his head. They knew this to be true; the Designer had said this to them in Eden. He had always treated them as friends. He honored every one of their choices, for good or for poor. And when they were poor, He never left them.

So Eve asked one more question, "Lord, will you find him and tell him how much we love him?"

"Yes, Eve, that I will do. How he responds and what he does is entirely up to him. His story is his to write, and the choices he makes now, will determine the outcome."

Adam, then, moved gently towards the Desigenr and Eve. Joining the embrace, he allowed his tears to fall. The Designer held them powerfully in His strong arms. He closed His eyes, and I watched as His glow flowed gently into them. His love was doing more for them at this moment than they could see or comprehend; it was beginning to heal and restore them again. They had felt this before, but right now, all they could feel was loss.

After what seemed an age, He released them. Adam then held Eve with such gentleness and love. Everyone who gathered could see the Designer's glow had stayed with them both. Such moments are sacred and will not be forgotten by any who saw this.

Turning to me, the Designer said, "Come Eagle, let us go find Cain."

CHAPTER 23

As I spread my wings and took flight, I looked back to see Eve collapse into Adam's arms. Her grief had stolen all of her strength. I wondered how I would have coped if it had been Wisdom lying dead and not Abel. It was a thought that made me shudder and made me realize how much I loved Wisdom. So great was the grief that I felt it now had a voice. The words of the Designer kept coming back to me, "If there was no grief, there was no love."

The Designer was walking below, and I wanted to ask Him a question about the design of love. He looked up at me and gave me a sad and yet, a warm smile. Can He read every one of my thoughts? Is He that connected to me?

He smiled even more at that and loudly said, "Yes."

Such joy flows into me every time He does something like this. One time when I was sitting with Him, He said, "Eagle, I know everything about you. I know how many feathers are on that powerful body of yours. I know your comings and goings. I love how you seek to understand. I love every one of your questions; your curiosity knows no bounds."

Well, today, many questions were flowing through my mind. For now, though, there was only one I wanted to ask: "My Lord, why is grief so painful?"

"Eagle, do you remember when I explained to you the strength of the bond that happens when Adam and Eve are connected by love?"

"Yes, my Lord. You said it was a dynamic, powerful, and vital kind of love. I remember you telling Adam and Eve about its bond, and it was so strong that the two of them became one."

The Designer smiled at that. I knew it was a memory that was precious to Him, and I could even imagine Him replaying it in His mind as He walked.

"Yes, Eagle, and that is the reason grief can be so painful. When two are united into one, the separation is very difficult. This bond is not just for a man and a woman to have; it is what happens when two people love each other well. You have felt this, Eagle. When Wisdom is close to you, I know you have felt this bond."

It was true, I do feel that, and even now, I wonder where she is and long for her to fly with me.

The Designer replied, "She is ahead of us, Eagle. You will see her soon; she is watching over Cain."

I laughed at that. He knows my thoughts; it seems I do not even need to speak.

"Ah, but Eagle, I love to hear you speak."

Then He continued, "Eagle, grief is not an evil thing. If anything, grief is a healing thing, which makes it a part of your design. When relationships end, and losses happen, grief helps guide a person to healing. I did this with you all those years ago, sitting under *The Tree of Life*. When I asked you to put your talons into the ground, you first doubted me, but soon you trusted me. When you felt the pain, you doubted me again. When you were able to move through the pain, you then felt my healing, and the trust grew."

He continued, "Grief is felt differently in every person. Think about what you felt and witnessed back at Adam's home. There was anger, fury, sadness, despair, numbness, denial, and even acceptance. You saw that in Adam when he was at Cain's workshop, and you will see it when we see Cain soon. None of this can be rushed, and each feeling needs to be expressed. Some of those feelings even happen simultaneously. It can be very confusing to those going through it, as we are now."

After a short while, he continued, "The pain of loss is so great, Eagle, because of the greatness of the love I created them by. The loss cannot be replaced, but the pain can be healed."

I pondered this for a long time as the Designer walked, and I flew above. We had traveled through the evening; neither of us was tired. With all the Designer had just revealed to me, how could I even want to sleep? Thoughts would come rushing in, and I pulled away to soar so I could be alone with my thoughts. Then questions would come flooding back in as a response to my thoughts, and I would plummet back down to ask them. This was a time I did not want to merely watch; I wanted to see, and I wanted to understand grief.

"Feeling the grief, Eagle, is a key to healing the pain." As He said this, He smiled to Himself as if He was recalling another memory. Then He continued, "Love is not love if choice is not freely and totally given. It is the riskiest and most powerful thing you can do at any one time. My greatest risk was creating Adam and Eve and giving them this choice. I could have withdrawn that choice and made them obey me, but what kind of relationship would that be? That would have made me their master. I did not want to rule them; I wanted to love them and to be loved by them. When I gave them choice, I invited them to give me that same choice, too."

There was so much wonder in what He had just spoken to me. Again, it was like I was listening to the mysteries of the Designer.

There was so much to think through, but someone was catching my attention way ahead.

"Eagle, look ahead. Do you see Wisdom?"

"My Lord, I have been seeing her for a long time, and she has seen me."

The Designer smiled at this. He was always so joy-filled when His design was working, and I loved feeling His design in me.

"I have felt her presence grow within me ever since we left Adam's home."

CHAPTER 24

I could see Wisdom circling the same location. It was still a long way off for a person walking, but I could already see she was marking the place where Cain had stopped. He was a long way from home and alone in the desert. We were now far west of Eden, and I could see Cain looked dirty and disheveled, like he had been wandering aimlessly for the past two days.

Wisdom continued to circle. I know she had seen me, but her commission was to watch over Cain, and she would not leave him. I could see she was tired, and it would not be long before I would be there to relieve her.

The Designer had gone silent; His eyes fixed on Cain. Whatever was to happen next with Cain was a mystery to me. However, I knew He loved him, and within His love was great mercy. Now He carried His mercy as if it was water to a man lost in the desert.

Soon Cain saw the Designer coming towards him. He made no effort to run or hide. Not that there was anywhere to hide out here. Cain looked like a defeated man without the energy to defend himself. It was then I noticed, high above Wisdom, that vultures were circling. Wisdom was all that stood between the vultures and the helpless form of Cain on the ground. The direness of Cain's situation was painfully obvious. I could hear the vultures chattering to themselves; their voices were somehow familiar. Then suddenly, I realized what I was hearing: the harsh voice of the talking snake. That wretched thing had spoken of legions of them, and now I could see what it meant.

While Wisdom was there, they would not dare come close to Cain. Wisdom was formidable, and it would have been a fool's errand to attack her or Cain. As the Designer came closer to Cain, He looked up and said, "Be gone." At that, they broke from their circling and flew further west.

The Designer broke from a walk into a run. There was an urgency within him, and he hurried to get to Cain. I could see now that Cain was dying, and his spirit was fading. Without help, he would soon join Abel.

When we arrived, Wisdom landed heavily on the ground; such was her exhaustion.

"How long have you been up there?" I asked her.

"Nearly two days," she replied through labored breathing. "I don't know how much longer I could have stayed up there. And those vultures. Could you hear them, Eagle? They sounded like that strange lizard."

I nodded at her, "Yes, Wisdom, I heard them. I have learned much over the past two days, and the Designer has opened my eyes to many things."

Although she was tired, she simply smiled at me and said, "This makes me so happy to hear He has done this. Now we can truly be one."

By now, the Designer had arrived, and in one movement, He scooped Cain up and held him to His chest; He could not hide His love for Cain. I could hear Him speaking words, but they were for Cain's ears alone. As each word landed in his ears, I could see life

come back into Cain's body. Little by little, I saw him flicker back
to life. His eyes filled with tears at one point, and he started to
weep. I could hear him whispering, "I'm sorry. I did not mean to
kill you."

It was then the memory of hearing Abel's voice at his grave
hit me like a thunderclap from the heavens. Abel is within the
Designer. Was Abel speaking to Cain through the Designer? Was
this what was causing Cain's life to flow again?

The Designer stood holding Cain close. As we watched, we saw
a glow flow from the Designer and gently into Cain. After a few
minutes, the Designer whispered, "Cain, why are you here?"

Cain's voice was cracked and dry. It could have been from
being out here without water, and it could have been the remorse
and grief he had been carrying. He simply said, "I killed him."

There was a long silence as the Designer held him, and then
Cain spoke again, "I deserve to die ... I came here to die."

Lifting Cain up off the ground, the Designer turned to Wisdom
and me and said, "Come, we need to find water."

Although Wisdom was tired nearly to the point of collapse, she
knew that she also needed water. Once again, she unfurled her
mighty wings and took flight, and we headed east.

We flew ahead of them; there was little talking on our flight to
the river. Wisdom only had eyes for the great Euphrates River. By
the time we arrived, it was well into the afternoon, and the sun had
lost much of its heat. It was a blessed relief to be there. Wisdom
just dove straight into the water and drank her fill. Seeing her do
this brought such relief to my spirit. I did not realize the tension
I had been carrying for her. Seeing how the water had revived her
brought a fresh wave of joy to my spirit. So much so that I began to
laugh. It nearly felt wrong to laugh, but such was the joy of seeing
Wisdom safe brought it bubbling out of my weary and grieving
spirit. She had fulfilled her commission, and we were one.

As the sun was setting, the Designer arrived at the bank of the river. This was His favorite time of day, but all that seemed to be lost on Him as He walked straight into the river holding Cain. The coldness of the water startled Cain awake, but he was still hovering somewhere between life and death. The Designer stood with him in His arms and allowed the river's water to flow over Cain. Dust and dirt were being washed away, and life was flowing back through him. The Designer gently scooped a little water into Cain's mouth. His first sip of water made him splutter, and most of it came straight back out of his mouth, along with all the dirt and dust in there. The Designer continued to scoop a little of the water, and each time Cain was able to drink a little more. Slowly, moments drifted by, and I could see Cain was slowly grasping who had him and where he was.

He had no defense and offered none; remorse is what Wisdom and I could see. Just watching him reminded me of his parents hiding among the bushes and covering themselves with fig leaves. He wanted to disappear; he wanted to be invisible. Although he was clothed, he was naked. He wanted to hide from the Designer, but he could not.

Eventually, the Designer brought him out of the water. By then, it was night, the day's warmth had now fled, and the evening's cool was turning cold. The Designer went and found wood for a fire and food to eat. As He built the fire and prepared a meal, Cain said nothing. By the time the food was ready, Cain was dry again, but he could not look at the Designer and just sat slumped with his head bowed.

"Cain," the Designer said, "I am not here to take your life; I am here to restore your life."

Whatever Cain was expecting, it was not that. He stirred, and his eyes widened in surprise, yet he still said nothing. All that could be heard now was the fire crackling and nighttime creatures awakening all around us. Wisdom and I sat together in a nearby tree, listening to it all. I know Wisdom has foresight, but I wondered if even this was beyond what she could see of Cain's future. Cain remained silent, and my mind started to wonder and take in the beauty of the Designer's creation. From the peace I gained from sitting beside Wisdom to gazing into the heavens. Above us, there was an endless array of stars that seemed to multiply as the night deepened. Counting them would have been impossible, yet the Designer had placed every one of them up there. As it was all quiet below, I wondered even further. I wondered how long it would take me to fly to those stars and what I would discover when I got there. My wonderings were then interrupted by the Designer's voice.

"What did you do, Cain?"

A very long silence followed this question, but the Designer was in no rush. He already knew the answer to the question, and I guess He asked it to see if Cain would own his story.

Eventually, Cain spoke, "I killed my brother; I killed Abel."

This again was followed by much more silence, which, again, the Designer was content to wait in. The next words that came from Cain were mixed with pain and anger, and they were directed at the Designer. "You favored him over me. Ever since you made us leave Eden, this has been your way. You accepted his gifts, but mine, you refused." Again, there was more silence, and the Designer did not even look like He was going to respond to the accusations.

"I had had enough," exclaimed Cain. "If I could not compete with him, then I would hurt him. I did not mean to kill him. I wanted your attention, but you gave me your back."

The last words had lost their sting. Cain was hurting, grieving, angry, and physically near death. Silence followed this, and the only noises we heard were those that were happening around us, not from any spoken voice. So, we waited.

The Designer then gently said, "How did you kill him?"

At that, Cain's head dropped again, and tears started to flow. He eventually found his voice and said so softly, "I did not mean to kill him. I only meant to confront him." More silence followed before he continued, "I was angrier than I have ever been before. That talking snake," he exclaimed. "That talking snake convinced me I deserved better. It convinced me that Abel had much more than I did. It convinced me that my parents loved him more than me. It convinced me I worked a cursed land while Abel worked a blessed land."

After another long silence, the Designer said, "I have dealt with the voice of the snake, Cain, and I know how persuasive it can be. Its task was to seed doubt within you, and in this, it succeeded. This seed gave birth to comparison, and comparison has birthed judgment. This judgment has birthed anger within you. I warned you that anger would give birth to hatred, and you would do things you would regret."

We were deep into the night now, but still, nothing rushed the Designer. He was content to wait and for Cain to understand that He wasn't going to abandon him. I could see that Cain needed to feel His presence. Occasionally, the Designer would get up and find wood for the fire. At some point in the night, Cain had drifted off to sleep.

It was well after sunrise when Cain stirred, and when he did, he was startled awake. It looked as if he was unsure where he was and was attempting to get his bearings. Then came the realization the Designer was still there. Cain looked like a startled animal, uncertain whether he was safe or caught. Finding his voice took him a while, but he eventually said, "My Lord, I have had a dream."

The Designer picked His head up and said, "Who was in your dream?"

The answer shocked him afresh. The Designer did not ask, 'What was your dream?' He asked, 'Who was in your dream?'

After the shock subsided, Cain said, "Abel was in my dream, and he was alive. He came to me and told me he forgave me."

The Designer replied, "And he has."

Again, Cain's shock could not be hidden. "How can this be? I killed him."

Even saying these words made Cain's heartbreak, and tears fell from his eyes again.

"Cain," He said. "Abel is alive, but not as you once knew him. Yes, his body has died, but you cannot kill his spirit. His spirit is with me, and last night in your dream, he told you that you are forgiven. But he said more than that, didn't he?"

"Yes," Cain said through tears. "He told me he loved me."

"And he does, Cain. As do your parents," He added.

At that, Cain looked up, and there was such pain in his eyes. The further realization of the pain this one act had brought fell on him. Sorrow and grief collided in his spirit and drove him back to his shame. He buried his head in his arms, and I could tell he wanted to hide eternally. So heavy was the grief at this moment that Wisdom and I could feel it like a force from where we were sitting. It again showed to me the pain of how one act could affect so many people, changing the course of their lives.

I did not have any words to say that could ease Cain's pain, and maybe that is the point. The pain was not to be eased; it had to be felt for it to heal. But what would healing look like for one who carried such a wound?

Cain, through tear-filled eyes, slowly looked up at the Designer and asked, "My Lord, what can I do?"

The Designer looked at him with such love in His eyes; His heart was also breaking. Cain could see that this act also affected the Designer. He was not above such emotional pain; He was completely and intimately connected to it. I could see He, too, was suffering from the pain that Abel's death had caused.

It was then a strange wondering entered my mind: could Cain's love heal the Designer? What does our love do to Him? Does it affect Him as His love does for us? Is this what it means to be love? Does the Designer have wounds?

The Designer said to him, "Cain, place your hands into the ground. I know I have asked you to do this many times, and just about as many times, you turned away from me. This time, though, I am inviting you again to place your hands into the ground. Your bothers blood has flowed into the ground by your hands. That was many miles from where we are now, but it is the same ground. The ground carries more than you know, and to me, it has a voice. When I saw Abel lying on the ground, it was his blood that called to me. In his blood was his life."

I had often witnessed when He asked Cain to do this. I was there when the Designer met with him shortly after they left Eden. Cain was young and saw no point in doing this. He blamed his pain on his parents. He would not put his hands into the ground for anything other than to make it produce his crops.

This day was different, though. Gone was the arrogance of the young man, and in its place was a completely broken man. When the Designer asked him to reach into the ground, he reached in and did it this time. The Designer's hands were already in the ground as well, awaiting Cain's response.

"Cain, your brother's blood cries out to you as well. This is not to be feared, for you have already heard his voice and his love for you; even though you have done this to him, he does not want you to carry the shame for another day."

Cain was trembling as his hands went deeper into the soil. As he did, I remembered the searing pain that went through me as I reached into the soil and felt the pain of my own shame. The Designer told me back then that it would take courage to reach through the pain to take hold of the love that flowed through all things. My prayer was that today, Cain would be courageous.

"Cain, what are you seeing and what are you feeling?" He asked.

The trembling had turned to outright shaking. I could tell that everything in Cain wanted to let go of what he was touching; I could see he was replaying in his mind what he had done.

"My Lord, there is too much blood; there is too much pain. I can no longer bear to hold this; there is too much pain. The bleeding won't stop. There is nothing I can do to make it stop." Cain cried.

At that, he pulled his hands from the ground and collapsed; he was weak and tired, and he was instantly asleep in front of the Designer.

Turning to me, the Designer said, "Eagle, what do you see?"

"My Lord, I see a man who is weak of body and spirit," I replied.

"Do you think he has the courage to be healed?" the Designer asked me in return.

I had long ago learned that when the Designer asked me a question, as he did to Cain, it was not because He didn't know the answer. He wanted to know if I knew the answer.

"My Lord, only you have the foresight to know the answer to your question. What I know is, only love will restore this man, and today, Cain has felt your love, and I think you have felt his."

"Well answered, Eagle. Later, we will discover if this is true. For now, we will let him sleep."

CHAPTER 25

Cain awoke many hours later in the day. He still looked like he needed to sleep for days before I would recognize the Cain I once knew. He appeared to have aged many years in the space of a few days.

"Cain, get up, wash yourself, and eat. Once you have done all of this, then we will meet here again," the Designer said.

As Cain did this, the Designer set about building another fire. He went out among the trees and brought back armload after armload of firewood. Once He lit the fire, he tended it and made sure it was well-lit by the time Cain returned.

Cain was clean and looking fresher than when he left. He found a space near the fire and sat close to the Designer. We could feel such love flow from the Designer; He was eager to connect with Cain. Healing was on his mind, and love was flowing from him, into the ground, and into Wisdom and me.

"Cain, you have been wandering these past few days, but in truth, for many years you have wandered from me. This day I am giving you the opportunity to return to me. Abel's physical life cannot be returned to you, and your actions still stand as ones that have caused much harm to you, your family, and your people. They cannot be undone, but there can be healing."

Cain sat as still as a stone. He was unmoved; it was impossible to tell what he was thinking. Was this another part of grief? Was he so disconnected from the Designer that he could not feel His love? Had Abel's or the Designer's words meant nothing to him? Had he forgotten what he felt when he put his hands into the ground?

Finally, he spoke, "You are going to cast me out of your presence, aren't you?"

The Designer said nothing; He just waited, sensing that more was yet to come.

"Who will protect me if I am sent from your presence? I will die out there, so why not just kill me now?"

It all started to make sense to me now. I had seen the same thoughts in Adam and Eve many years ago. Like theirs, Cain's mind was a battlefield, and fear had taken hold of him. It was as if he could no longer see yesterday's hope of restoration. Had he been so long away from the Designer's love that he could not comprehend His mercy? Could he only believe for punishment? Yesterday he felt the magnitude of the pain in the ground, and now, today, he did not believe that much pain could be healed. It did not take long, but he had lost hope. In doing so, he could not allow himself to work through the grief and pain or take hold of the love the Designer had for him. So great was the deception that he believed death was the only way out.

"No, Cain. Again, I did not come here to kill you. To kill you would go against everything about my character and design. To kill you would be to kill a part of me. Your physical life is safe and will continue to be. What I want to heal is the little boy within you who cried out to me earlier, the one who wants to be seen and heard. Long ago, you lost your voice. You were forced from a garden you called your home. Everything changed on the fateful

146

day you and Abel found that watering hole. You ran to tell your parents about it, but you did not find them. Hiding in their shame was where you eventually discovered them. You could do nothing about it. It was not your fault, nor was it your choice."

The Designer did not give Cain an opportunity to respond.

"By the time you were old enough to be responsible for your choices, that little confused boy was no longer seen. The playful boy who ran through Eden, exploring every corner of it, is hidden deep down inside of you. That little boy wanted his father's attention when you brought in your first harvest. You wanted to hear, 'well-done son,' but instead, you saw your father and me praise Abel for the success of his flock. It was that little boy who again wanted his father to notice when you bent the mighty Euphrates River to give you the water to irrigate many fields. But again, all you saw was a father captivated by Abel's efforts. Each disappointment took you further and further from him and also from me. You gave me less and less time. You no longer looked for me in the cool of the evening. Do you remember the times I would come to your workshop, and you said that you were too busy to walk with me? Do you remember your gifts to me were getting less and less each year? Do you remember what you told Enoch to do in gathering the gift for this year's giving?"

He continued, "You did not even want to be there with me. You wanted it to happen like a duty or a ritual so that you could get to eating and drinking. Cain, you can blame the talking snake. You can point out the failings of your parents. But this is all behind you now. Now you are carrying a shame you believe cannot be lifted and cannot be healed. For this to be true, it would mean your shame is where your hope runs out. Cain, hear me today, hopelessness is the voice of death. This is where death takes over, and all you can hear is that you deserve to die. But death is never the last voice around me. For it to be so would mean death is more powerful than life. It would mean hatred is more powerful than love. Neither of these is true, Cain. You once believed these things, and today, I am asking you to, once again, believe in me."

The Designer's words had silenced Cain. Moments ago, he was defiant and resolved to an outcome that was worse than death. Now he simply sat and listened to the Designer's voice. I could see His words were sinking into Cain. Before our eyes, I watched as a softness returned to his spirit.

"Cain, can you imagine the *two trees* in Eden?" He asked.

Cain simply nodded. His words had all dried up.

"Imagine yourself sitting there. Which *tree* are you sitting under?"

"My Lord, it has been so long since I tasted the fruit of the *Tree of Life* I no longer remember its flavor."

"You did not know the taste of the fruit from *The Tree of Knowledge of Good and Bad*, but you know its scent. You can still smell the aroma of that *tree*, can't you?"

"Yes, my Lord, I can."

Silence followed these words, but the Designer could see he had a question.

"What is your question, Cain?"

"Why can I remember the smell of that *tree*, but I cannot remember the taste of the fruit from *The Tree of Life*?"

"You would remember it if you would choose to sit with me and place your hands into the ground. Because you have not done so for many years, you have found yourself wondering about the taste of the *tree* you could not eat from. You let go of the life that flowed from the *tree* I gave you all access to. The *Tree of knowledge of Good and Bad* is still in Eden, and its fruit has continued to cry out to you."

"You believed the same lie your mother accepted. She was convinced I was withholding my love from her, as you have now done. But, Cain, I was not withholding my love from her, and I am not withholding it from you. To do so would be to withhold all of my goodness from you, and Cain, you have truly seen and known my goodness in these years. The ground has yielded its crops, yes, and you have prospered. I know you have worked hard, but you did not create the soil, the seed, the sun, the seasons, or the water. Even though you turned your back on me, I did not ever turn my back on you. Even in your rebellion, my love still flowed to you."

The Designer's words were wearing Cain down. The stone-like features that were there minutes before were continuing to change. He was softening as the Designer's words fell on him. There was not a hint of condemnation in His voice; every word was an invitation to healing. Again, I could see how much He loved Cain.

"Cain, it is time for the little boy to heal. He has not been abandoned, but I realize it has felt that way. He was not able to receive my love because he feared being sent from my presence for something he did not do. He worked hard so he did not have to rely on anyone. His focus became safety, not love. It is time for him to feel my love," the Designer said gently.

"My Lord, I have much to learn," Cain said. "Can my shame be truly healed?"

"Yes, Cain, it can. This healing, though, will take courage and time. The wounds that have been created run deep and cannot be fixed in an instant. But I will not leave you; indeed, there is no place that you can run from me. If you choose to heal, then today will begin a restoration that will span generations."

"So, you will give me your mercy?" Cain whispered.

"Yes, Cain, you have all of my mercy," the Designer said. "My mercy will be a mark on you, Cain. All who see it will know that I have marked you, and no one will harm you because of this mark."

"My Lord, what does the mark look like?" Again, Cain's voice was only a whisper.

"Tomorrow, if you are willing, you will receive it. For now, you need sleep."

CHAPTER 26

Cain awoke suddenly from another dream. He was sweating and appeared to have been crying. Again, it took him a few moments to get his bearings. Beside him, the Designer had sat the whole night. He hadn't left Cain's side.

"What did you dream, Cain?" the Designer gently said.

"I dreamt of my mother. She was crying."

"And I dreamt of my father. He was angry; he was in my workshop throwing all of my tools around."

"Then, I dreamt of Abel. He was being laid in a stone cave, and a great stone had been placed across the opening to seal him into the rock."

"I also dreamt of Miriam ... she is carrying a child within her."

Cain looked bewildered by everything he had dreamt. He stared into the fire and spoke as if he was talking to it. Eventually, he broke his gaze and turned to the Designer.

"My Lord, what does all of this mean?"

"You have seen the past," the Designer said. "But there was more to the dream, wasn't there?"

"Yes, my Lord," he replied. "I dreamt I was wandering alone through the wilderness, and a glorious light shone from within me. All who saw me knew I was marked by you. No one would dare to harm me."

He then continued, "I also dreamt the land would no longer produce what it once did for me." Cain's voice had trailed off as he said this. "My Lord, I know the meaning of this dream. I was once so proud of my work; so proud I thought I no longer needed you. I had taken for granted your creation and your goodness. My Lord, I know I am no longer a farmer."

"Cain, ahead of you is a time of wandering. A time when you will feel homeless but will not be hopeless. This will be a time of discovery; you will discover who you are and all I have designed you to be. There is a family and a city for you to build. From you will come generations who will make music and create the tools for building. Your name will be great, but you will be known for the mark you carry. But also know this; I will never leave you."

The Designer paused before He continued, "The day will also come when you will be restored to your parents and the generations that will come from them."

At that, Cain broke down and wept. Up until the night before, he had readied himself for the Designer's justice, not His mercy. His actions showed he knew he deserved to die. But, here, he found the Designer's judgment did not look like what he had expected. And it was not what I had expected.

Wisdom leaned over and said, "It would be the Designer's mercy that would heal Cain's shame. It would be His mercy that would begin a healing work that would span the generations. It would be His mercy that would confound every work of the strange lizards, talking snakes, or waiting vultures."

Cain moved away from us all and wept for what seemed an age. His tears of grief intermingled with tears of relief. We sat in the midst of another sacred moment.

Wisdom again leaned across to me and whispered, "I believe Cain is emptying himself of all the tears he has stored up for many years. He longs to go back in time and change all he has done, but he knows he can not. His past will be like a thorn in his flesh that will continue to cause him pain until the healing work of the Designer's love has run its course."

The Designer had been silent through all the tears; indeed, there were tears in His own eyes as He watched one He loved so much endure such grief. He had turned back to the fire and tended it with a stick to stir the embers back to a flame. To me, it looked symbolic of what He was doing for Cain. The flame of love was now being seen.

After many minutes, He called to Cain, "Come and sit closer to me."

Cain got up and moved to sit directly opposite the Designer. He struggled to look Him in the eye, but he had positioned himself right in front of Him to start his healing journey.

"Cain, come around and sit beside me. Come, place your hands into the ground with me."

Cain moved to sit beside him, and once he was comfortable, he closed his eyes and sat in silence for many more minutes. He hesitated to place his hands into the ground.

He said, "My Lord, I have touched the pain that is there; it is more than I can bear."

The Designer replied, "I know, Cain, which is why I will bear it for you and with you. Place your hands into the ground, and I will show you my love."

Cain tentatively did as he was asked. The trembling was back, and he was readying himself to feel the pain that had rendered him unconscious the day before. It was Wisdom who spoke next, in such low tones that Cain could not hear, "Remember, Eagle, you are not here to watch; you are here to see."

I closed my eyes and saw the most extraordinary vision. I could see Cain's hands in the ground. The pain was still there, and I could see it as if it was pulsing from deep within the ground. He was sensing it, but he was not feeling the pain it. I opened my eyes, and I could see the Designer was in excruciating pain. The pain was affecting every part of His body. I think He was feeling all the pain Cain had experienced, the disappointments, the rejections, and the abandonment. I closed my eyes, and once again, my vision blazed to light. I realized I could see Abel again, but I was back at his lifeless body in the field. I could hear Abel's blood crying out to the Designer. Abel's cries were not only a voice to Him; they were a deep pain. In vision, I watched as the Designer's face contorted. I even felt the pain as if it was searing heat on my face. As I opened my eyes, I could see that Cain could see it as well, but he did not know what to do. For him to see the extent of the Designer's love was more than he could bear.

He cried out, "No, my Lord. Let me receive the pain, not you. It is not yours to take."

The Designer responded, "As I receive your great pain, so you now receive my mercy and my love."

At that great cry, the Designer slumped to the ground, but as he did, He looked into Cain's eyes and whispered, "It is finished."

Cain sat staring at his hands. He had pulled them from the ground when he had cried out to the Designer. As he stared into his hands, something beautiful happened; his hands started to glow. I had seen this before in Abel. The glow in his hands then started growing and could now be seen throughout his body. From his hands, it traveled to his arms and into his torso. From there, it went into his legs until finally into his head, and eventually, his whole body glowed.

Wisdom and I sat there and stared at this phenomenon. Whatever Cain had thought the outcome of this moment was going to be, it was not this. How Cain's life had changed in the past few days, and here, it changed again. Not long ago he thought he would be banished and marked out as one the Designer abandoned. That could not be further from the truth. He was marked by the Designer's glory that would draw people to him, not drive people from him.

Cain stood up and marveled at what he was seeing as well. He could not see all of himself, but what he saw took his breath away. I do not think he could have imagined anything like this.

Wisdom sat beside me, simply and repetitively saying, "Wow, wow, wow."

It was then my attention went to the Designer, He was still slumped on the ground. Exhaustion was written all over his face and body. He had a slight smile on His face, but there was still much pain there. I motioned to Wisdom, who immediately flew to the ground to be with Him. She sunk her talons into the ground and whispered to the Designer, "I love you." As she spoke the words, I could see some of the discomfit lift from him, so I, too, flew to the ground and did the same.

A powerful lesson was happening right in front of us. The Designer is love, and our love is what He needed. Cain, too saw this unfolding in front of him, and just like the Designer did for him, he came and held the Designer in his arms and allowed their love to intermingle. I could see the glow flowing from Cain, and back into Him. The pain was healing, and once again I witnessed the restorative power of love.

"My Lord?" I asked, "Do you love me?"

The Designer could not help but laugh. It hurt him to do so, but joy was there. "Yes, Eagle, you know I love you."

"Rest in our love, my Lord," I said.

He smiled again, and I could sense Him relaxing into Cain's arms. Who would ever believe what I was seeing? Who could fully understand His love? I discovered it in the most surprising of places.

"My Lord, do you love me?" I asked again.

The Designer breathed deeply and said, "Yes, Eagle, you know I love you."

"Receive our love, my Lord," I said.

As I spoke it, He exhaled the breath that He had taken in, and in the act of receiving our love, He breathed in so deeply that I am certain He breathed in air that the three of us had just exhaled.

"My Lord, can I be bold enough to ask one more question?" I said.

"Yes, Eagle, I have called you my friend and told you that you can ask anything you like?"

"My Lord, do you love Cain?" I asked.

I knew that He did. I just wanted Cain to hear it. Wherever Cain's wanderings would take him, and whatever city he would build, he would be able to cling to the very words that were about to come from the Designer.

At that, the Designer raised himself up to look straight into Cain's eyes again. "Cain," the Designer said. Cain still struggled to hold His gaze for too long, but the Designer's words caused him to look deeply into Him. "Today, I have marked you with my mercy, my love, and my glory. There are no greater gifts I can give you than these. They are eternal, and they will guide and protect you through this next stage of your life. As they are with you, so am I. I am love, which means the love that you feel is me and will not be taken from you. Enduring your pain is only a small portion of the love I am still to impart to you. I love you, Cain. Look for me in the cool of the evening. I will meet you there."

I thought that Cain's tears had run dry, but I was wrong. But these were not tears of sadness; they were tears of joy. The Designer was crying the same tears, and once again. Wisdom and I were both profoundly impacted by what we witnessed.

The rest of the day, the Designer and Cain spent together. Wisdom and I could see they were now deep in a conversation that was just for the two of them. Even though this day had been extraordinary for Cain, I knew there would be moments, times, and even seasons when the voice of shame, would remind him of all he had lost and what he had done. I had known my own shame, and it had become like a thorn in my side that I could not remove. It was the Designer's grace and mercy that healed what I could not fix.

So, leaving them to their conversation, Wisdom and I took to the skies. To soar again was life-giving. It had felt like it had been weeks since we had done so, but truly, it had only been a few days. As we soared high above, we both spoke our stories of all we had seen and witnessed. Wisdom asked me to repeat the entire story from when the Designer and I met with Adam and Eve to when we saw the vultures in the sky. I knew her foresight would have given her much of this, but I know she desired to hear it from what I had 'seen.'

As we soared, we moved out further and further in ever-widening circles. Far to the east and out of our sight, Adam and Eve were waiting for news from us. I knew Eve would watch the horizon every day hoping for a glimpse of Cain. A pang of sadness moved through my body when I realized this would not be happening when she desired it.

As we soared, our conversation shifted from what had been, and into what could be. It was inspiring to talk about the days ahead of us and to imagine all that would be revealed to us by the Designer. But it was also incredible to think of how much had changed in such a short space of time, and then wonder of all that could be in the days ahead of us. We both missed Abel. The space in our lives he held would not be filled by anyone. He was a man to follow, and a man who loved well.

It was evening by the time we returned to the Designer and Cain. When we arrived, they were cooking a meal, and it was as if the conversation had just continued the whole day. Cain was alive now, and the glow within him was as strong as the glow that I had seen so often in Abel. I knew we were witnessing the Designer's love operating in the fullness of its design. There was no condemnation and no shame here; there was just love.

Our final evening together was one of gentleness and grace. The pain of the days previous had not disappeared, but much of the shame had. It reminded me of the days with Adam and Eve after they left Eden. Back then, there were times of incredible joy and laughter, and then there were times of heaviness and sadness. Over time, I could sense the rhythm of these patterns. Now I thought of them as if they were a dance I would always be learning. This rhythm of healing would come to Cain, but it would take time, and it would take courage.

That night, Cain said his goodbyes to us all. The Designer smiled at him and said, "Tomorrow, I will look for you in the cool of the evening. And also, Cain, I will send your family to you; your wife and children will be reunited with you."

The next morning, we awoke to silence. Cain had left during the night.

CHAPTER 21

Wisdom and I took to the skies as the sun rose. It was a beautiful time of day to fly as everything was fresh, and the sky was ours to play in. The Designer had farewelled us back at the river. We would see Him again with Adam and Eve. He told us He wanted to visit Miriam before He met with them.

Miriam needed His words and His love. But more than this, she needed His presence. There was not a time she had met with the Designer without Abel. All of this was so new and so painful. Even thinking about it brings tears to my eyes. They shared such a beautiful bond. All who saw them could see the love they carried for each other. Everyone knew if Abel was not out in the fields with the sheep, then he was always by Miriam's side.

He told us He would share with her Cain's remorse and restoration. I cannot imagine how she would take this news, as we all knew that Miriam was always wary of Cain. Whatever happened, we knew that Miriam's and the Designer's grief would be shared together in the cool of the evening.

As we soared high into the skies, my mind began to imagine this meeting between the two of them. I am sure He would invite her to place her hands into the ground with Him and feel His love in such deep ways. I wondered how deep He would take her. Would she be able to hold on through the pain, or would the Designer take the pain into Him, as he did with Cain? Would He allow her to see Abel, as I did? Would He even let Abel speak to her?

She would also be carrying Abel's child, a journey she would now walk alone. Her grief was deep, yet so precious was the child who grew within her. It was a pain I could not comprehend.

The Designer had also told us the child would carry his father's glow all the days of his life. It was easy for me to imagine this, yet at the same time, it was painfully hard to hold the vision. Abel walked daily with that glow, and seeing it in his child would be easy. But to see it knowing that the child's father is no longer with them, grieved every part of my spirit.

He told us that Miriam would not need to worry about protection or provision. When we asked if she would find another and if he would be the provider, the Designer merely smiled and said, "I have spoken it and it will be."

He loved Miriam.

CHAPTER 28

Wisdom and I returned to Adam and Eve's home long before the Designer. We were welcomed and met with curiosity about everything we had seen. However, we both knew the Designer wanted to meet with them and tell them personally what had happened. We simply let them know Cain was well and the Designer would be here in the morning.

I sensed the heaviness of grief in them both. To counter it, they were trying to keep busy. Adam had cut so much wood for the fire that I thought it would last many seasons. Eve had been readying the home, and she had even made a room for Cain. The very image of her doing this was heartbreaking to watch. I could already see Eve's heart would break again when the Designer told her Cain was not coming home.

Wisdom leaned over to me and said, "Eagle, what do you see?"

"Wisdom, I see a home that is being prepared for a son who will not return until he has finished wandering."

"What else?" she asked

"I see two grieving people who are enduring something they never have before. I see a couple who are trying to do the best they can, but in doing so, they look to distract themselves from the pain. If they keep doing this, they will slowly let go of the Designer's love." I paused to think of what I was seeding, then said, "The very thought of this did not come to me until I looked closely with my eyes. To everyone else, probably even themselves, they are doing the best they think they can, but busyness will keep them from rest and healing."

Wisdom looked at me, nodded, and said, "You have seen clearly, Eagle. If they do not choose to heal with love, they will try to heal with their knowledge and strength. This is such an important moment, and it is why the Designer wants to be here with them."

"Wisdom, we both know the power of the love that flows through Him; indeed, it flows through every living thing. And yet, we have both seen how easy it is for people to choose to reject His love."

I stopped and paused as a thought came to me and said, "To me, it seems too easy. The Designer has made His creation in such a way that it sustains itself. It reproduces itself, it has seasons, and life just naturally flourishes with His creation. Surely many will discover this truth and become like Cain was, no longer loving Him as He has loved them?"

Wisdom gave me a crooked smile. She knew what I was saying was true. "Eagle, there is much truth in what you are saying, but do not forget, His creation is dependent on His love. People may walk away for a time, but they will come back to Him. Some will be driven back by their needs, and others will choose to come back to Him on their own. Through it all, He will not stop loving them. As I said, His creation is dependent on His love. If He stopped loving them, then the creation would cease to exist. We would cease to exist."

"How do you know this? There has never been a time when His love hasn't existed."

"Exactly," Wisdom replied. "We cannot live in this world apart from His love. Whether or not people recognize it, it is here and will always be. You have just witnessed this with Cain; he cannot exist outside of the Designer's love. He even said it himself."

"This means that everything that has happened, is happening, and will happen will do so in and with His love."

She smiled at me and said, "Eagle, do you remember when the Designer first asked you if you wanted to be healed?" She continued without giving me an opportunity to respond, "To get to the healing, you had to move through the pain to discover His love. His love was an invitation into healing; then His love became your healing. It was present before, through, and after. All He asked you to do was to receive it. In saying 'yes' to Him, you allowed Him to love the areas of your pain, failure, shame, and loss you carried."

Wisdom's words were true. Ever since that strange lizard brought fear to Eden, I had encountered emotions I did not know existed. I had not even known what pain, failure, loss, shame, or death was; now, I do, and yet there was far more for me to know.

Then another thought came to me: Cain was Adam's son, and he walked away from the Designer. How easy would it be for those who had not spent time in Eden or with the Designer to walk away?

Wisdom was hearing my thoughts, "Eagle, do not think that the Designer has missed this. He did not create all of this, thinking it would die soon after it started. Remember what the Designer told you way back in Eden, '*You have been given the privilege of watching two of the most powerful forces that exist at work. The first is choice: the ability to choose to be in relationship with me. The second is love. When I get down from this tree and go find my beloved ones, you will see the beginnings of the greatest love story that has ever been known, and this time, no strange lizard will be able to stop it.'"*

"Eagle, these two great forces are still at work, and they will always be at work. Time will show how powerful they are. You wonder about how easy it is to walk away from the Designer. He will always be present with His creation, and He will always honor their choices. You have seen that now in Eden and also here with Cain. The Designer has told you He will never leave them, which means His love will always be present with them. This also means that there will be many more generations to come who get to encounter His love as we have encountered it. It will look different to each generation, and it will look different to each person. He loves each one uniquely. We will get the privilege of seeing this time and again."

CHAPTER 29

As the sun rose, the Designer appeared on the horizon. It was another beautiful morning. The dawn had given way to a beautiful sky of red that faded to orange. The air was fresh, but it was not cold; it was just the way I loved it. It was so good to see the Designer coming towards us. This was going to be a big day.

Eve soon saw Him, too, and ran toward Him. Soon she realized He was walking alone. I could see her shoulders slump and, it seemed, much of her hope. She slowed to the point of stopping, fell to her knees, and waited for the Designer.

When they met, they were too far away to hear what was being said, but Eve's face and tears told us the story when she turned towards home. The Designer walked slowly with her all the way. All of her urgency in getting out there to Him was now just a memory. Adam came out and greeted the Designer warmly, but obviously, this was not how he expected this homecoming to be, either.

I cannot even imagine what they must have been going through. Would I have wanted to see my son if he had killed my other son? Would I have forgiven easily? Would I have wanted to hold him? They must have had so many unanswered questions, and maybe they did not even want to ask some of them for fear of what the answer would be.

The Designer invited them both to come and gather around the fire while He built up the smoldering remains. I never recall Adam and Eve refusing an invitation from Him, but I could tell they were anxious about meeting with Him this time. Little was said while the Designer breathed upon the coals, bursting them back into flame. Once the flame grew, He slowly added more logs to the fire. He was in no rush.

The people who lived around them were curious about what the Designer would say, and they were also eager to know what had happened to Cain. I had heard some of them say that they could not believe Cain would do this to his brother. Others, though, firmly believed him to be guilty and deserved to give up his own life. Everyone, though, felt such sorrow for Adam and Eve. One son was dead, and the other was missing. Although their curiosity peaked, none of them dared invade this sacred space for them with the Designer.

Once the Designer was satisfied that the fire was well-lit, He came and sat close to Adam and Eve. He looked at them both with such love. Eve still seemed to hold a glimmer of hope that Cain would be here soon, but Adam looked like a man who was about to hear the worst news of his life.

The Designer breathed deeply and said, "Cain is well."

At that, Eve gasped and started to cry. She could no longer hold in the grief that had been welling up in her for days. She also wondered if Cain had killed Abel, he would surely have paid for his actions with his life. But she would have also known what the Designer had done for her.

"What I am about to tell you will hurt you, but for healing to happen, truth must be where we start." He allowed His words to sink in before He continued, "We found him a few days ago lost in the desert and very close to death. He was alone, exhausted, dehydrated, and starving. Wisdom had been watching over him at my request."

Adam looked up at Wisdom and, with tears in his eyes, simply nodded his thanks. Eve was still too consumed with her grief to look anywhere but down.

"There is much to the story you will want to know, and in time, it will all come out. What you need to know now is that Cain admitted he killed Abel. He was angry and jealous, and in that rage, the talking snake convinced him that his world would have been better without Abel in it. He did not mean to kill him."

The Designer continued, "He hit him with his digging tool."

A long silence followed as He again let these words sink into Adam and Eve. The only things we could hear were Eve's sobs and the fire's crackling. Each word that flowed from His mouth was filled with His love, but they were not the words Eve longed to hear. There was no condemnation in His voice, and He was simply conveying the facts to them.

Eventually, the Designer said, "Cain's remorse for what he has done was strong. He knew the severity of his actions and would do anything to have this time again." Another lengthy silence followed.

Eve's voice cracked as she said, "If he was sorry, and if he did not mean to kill him, then why did you not let him return?" It was barely more than a whisper, but it contained such a cry from her heart, and she wanted her only son left to be with her.

The Designer replied, "There is much for Cain to discover about himself. He is wandering the land of Nod while doing this. You both know he has been wandering for many years, and that will continue for a time as he heals."

Eve could not comprehend how this could solve the devastation that had just happened to her family, but she had no words, only tears, and sobs. Adam put his arm around her and cradled her head on his chest, which was soon wet with her tears.

"Eve, you will see your son again. But it will not be this day, this week, this month, or even this year. Do not fear for his safety, for he carries my mark upon him. No one will steal his life from you, for my presence is on him, and I will not leave him alone."

Again, the Designer paused and allowed His words to be heard and received. Adam and Eve were trying to comprehend, but so much had changed that could never be unchanged. Their family had been cracked wide open with a wound they must have feared was fatal to them all.

"Eve, do you remember the glow that flowed through Abel after he spent time with me?"

Eve whispered, "Yes, my Lord, I remember it well. It was the same glow Adam and I have seen in each other, but I rarely saw it in Cain."

Again, the last words were reduced to a whisper, as if saying them was pushing Cain further from them.

"Yes, Eve, you have spoken true. But what you do not know is Cain now carries that glow, and everyone can see it. I have marked him with my presence, and I could only do this because Cain desired to meet with me."

The air shimmered as the Designer spoke out these words. It felt like Adam and Eve had come fully alive again at that moment. I felt the excitement with Wisdom as she sat beside me. His words were, once again, creating life.

"Cain placed his hands into the ground and felt the love I have for him. He did not do this out of duty but from his desire to find me. This desire has added many things to his life, and he now knows how much I love him."

He then continued, "I have tasked him to build a city and told him that generations of people would come from him. He is no longer a farmer; those days are now behind him. The city he builds will produce carpenters, brickmakers, and all kinds of trades that will build other towns and cities. Even more than that, instrument makers and musicians will come from his city."

Eve was listening, but I'm wondering whether she heard anything other than that Cain would not be here this year. Adam, though, closed his eyes and looked to be trying to imagine all he had just heard.

"Giving you this news is not the only reason I am here with you," He said. He paused before continuing, "I am here to tell you Miriam is carrying Abel's child, and she will need you both."

At this, Eve's eyes blazed open, and for the first time, I could see the flicker of hope back in her. Her eyes were such a window into her soul. She could never hide her feelings, as her eyes would always give her thoughts away. It was the one part of her that no amount of fig leaves could hide.

"In four months, you will be grandparents again," said the Designer.

Adam and Eve just held each other and cried. New life would be given where their son's life was taken.

The Designer continued, "But this wasn't the only reason I returned. I came to help you heal."

"Many years ago, I walked with you and your family as you left Eden. Today, I will walk with you and your family again as you grieve all that has occurred. I will not leave you in your pain. There are better days ahead, but for the moment, we will take them one day at a time. Just like we once did. Abel is with me now. He is safe, and he is well. Cain is also with me, but not as Abel is with me. As I said, my mark is upon him, and he will go on and build a noble name for himself."

"Your healing is what I want to talk to you about. The pain and grief you feel are real, but they are not eternal. You may wonder how long you are able to survive with such pain in your hearts, but again, I assure you this pain is temporary and can be healed."

169

Adam and Eve were now listening intently. The day had not gone as they had hoped, but each word the Designer spoke gave them a little more hope.

"Close your eyes, and let me remind you of a time we sat together under *The Tree of Life*. Allow yourself to feel the ground beneath you and remind yourself of the extraordinary scent that the fruit from the tree gave off." He paused and invited them to remember. "Can you feel the breeze that was blowing that day? Can you see it gently moving the trees that surrounded us?" Again He paused for them to remember. "As always, when we were there together, it was at the time of day that we simply called the 'cool of the evening.' Can you both picture this?" asked the Designer.

The countenance on their faces changed as the Designer asked them to remember a time in Eden. It was beautiful to watch Adam and Eve return to Eden in their minds. I could tell that the Designer was avoiding the memory of the strange lizard. There was still more healing ahead for them with that memory, but for this moment, I could tell that *The Tree of Life* had captured their hearts again.

Adam said, "Yes, my Lord. I can see it clearly, and I wish more than anything that I could be back there with my boys."

Eve said, "Yes, my Lord, I can see it and feel it. My wish is I never touched that other *tree*, and we would all still be together if it weren't for that *tree*!"

The Designer allowed them to hold that vision for some time before He said, "Where is Abel in your vision?"

What an extraordinary moment to witness as they both beheld him in their vision. By this stage, I, too, had gone to *The Tree of Life* in my mind. Abel was there, and he was whole again.

Adam exclaimed, "He has come to sit with us, and he told us how much he loves us."

Eve also exclaimed, "I can hear him speaking to us as well. He is saying that He is safe."

The Designer said, "And safe he is. What you are seeing is true. Abel does still love you, and he is safe. He is no longer as you knew him in the flesh; he is now of the spirit. He now lives in me. You can see him any time you like by picturing yourself by the *Tree of Life*."

The Designer then asked, "Now, I want you to picture Cain in your mind. Can you see him?"

This time it was Eve that spoke first, "My Lord, I see him wandering that new land you spoke of, and he is glowing." Eve paused as she waited to see more, and what she saw troubled her, "But the land I see is harsh and looks very difficult for him to grow crops from. How will he survive in such a place?"

The Designer responded, "Again, you see clearly, Eve. He is indeed glowing. As I said, he does so because I have marked him with my love, my mercy, and my presence. All who see him will see me. He will no longer be a farmer, for he will be known as a builder of cities, and in that place, I will provide for him."

"Can I go to him, my Lord?" Eve asked.

"Eve, there is nothing withheld from you. You are free to go or to stay. The day I created you, I gave you the freedom to choose, and it is a freedom you will always possess." the Designer replied.

Adam, too, had seen the vision. This time it was he who wept.

The Designer quietly asked, "Adam, why are you weeping? What is happening for you?"

"My Lord, today I awoke expecting you to tell me that Cain was dead too or that he had been cast out of your presence. But now I see that you have placed your presence within him. Your love, indeed, knows no bounds. You have, yet again, shown me the wonder and power of your love." Adam replied.

"Adam, love is the healer, and I am love. It is who I Am. It would be against my character to kill him or cast him away from my presence. Adam, I love Cain. Let this be a revelation to you of who I am. I did not kill you or cast you away from me in Eden, and I will not do this with Cain."

He then continued, "The image of *The Tree of Life* is one that you have access to at any time. Your hearts need time to heal, and you will find healing there. Let each day be a day where my love can reach deeper within you and touch those parts of you that are so wounded. I am here to love you both well," then the Designer went silent for a time.

Finally, he said, "There is still another reason I came here." This time He smiled as He looked into Eve's eyes, "Eve, you are to have another son, and his name will be Seth, and he, too, will carry my mark and my love to the generations."

Eve gasped.

"He will never replace Abel. There is only one Abel, as there is only one Eve, one Adam, and one Cain. The glow you saw in Abel will be found in Seth and will remain for generations. Inside of your family, I have placed a seed that will eventually produce the fullness of life you found in Eden."

Once again, Eve gasped and then cried. Wisdom told me that Eve had wondered if she was pregnant a few days ago. But then, all of this had happened, and she must not have given it another thought. The uneasiness she had felt in her stomach must have been covered by the grief that had flooded her entire body.

"My Lord, how can I ever repay you for such a gift?" Eve exclaimed.

The Designer smiled and said, "A few days ago, Abel presented me with a gift. It was the most perfect lamb, and there was no defect in it. It was such a magnificent gift. Today, I am giving you a gift such as this. Your sons will carry my pleasure and my presence. I will love this son with the same love I loved Abel with and the same love I love Cain with."

They spoke of many more things that evening, and the conversation went deep into the night. The Designer's presence and love were beginning to heal them. It would take many years for the grief to heal, but I already sensed the new joy He brought. He loved them so much.

As I sat and watched, it reminded me of a time before a strange lizard had opened its mouth. I held the vision of the great *Tree of Life*. It was magnificent and laden with its incredible multi-colored fruit. It carried a scent that permeated every corner of Eden, and when the wind blew just right, I could even smell it outside of Eden.

CHAPTER 30

A few months later, Seth was born. He was the image of Abel, and he carried the glow of his brother as well, just like the Designer had said. He also loved to spend time with the Designer. Each afternoon, Seth would head to the banks of the Euphrates River to await the Designer.

He would spend hours with Him. Sometimes Eve would send me to get him for dinner. I think she realized it would be a difficult task. He never wanted to leave the Designer's presence. I loved to see Seth spending time with the Designer, and it did not bother them that I watched. Each of these encounters grew the brilliant light within Seth. And as those days turned into weeks, months, and years, Seth's children would discover the Designer's heart and the life He poured into all of His creation. They would discover His love flowed through the ground they stood on. They would discover a love they could build their lives on.

But for me ... one image continued to plague me ... the image of the dead *tree* remained.

EPILOGUE

From Seth would come many sons and daughters. Through one of his sons, many more generations would pass until finally came one named Noah. He carried the same glow as Abel and Seth, and it was glorious.

But that is a story for another time ...

AUTHOR NOTE

This book follows on from the success of the Eagle in *Eden's Blueprint*. The metaphor in the prologue and epilogue became an instant hit with readers, and I allowed myself to believe that maybe I could write fiction. So, I simply began writing. Initially, I was thinking of doing an overview of many of the Old Testament stories in one book. I wanted to attempt to see if I could culminate God's love through the Eagle's lens of Jesus' death, resurrection, and ascension. However, as I began writing, a wealth of imagined stories was developing, which bridged many places in scripture where so much of the story is missing. The story of Adam and Eve leaving Eden's and what happened to Cain was one of those.

You will notice that chapters 1 and 2 are versions of the prologue and epilogue from *Eden's Blueprint*. It made sense to me to include them in this story, as they provide the context for the rest of the book. Also, I thought this would be helpful for those who had not read *Eden's Blueprint*.

Bible readers would know that the Genesis story of Adam and Eve and their subsequent exit from Eden is completed within a few short chapters. Yet, it records these people living for hundreds of years. So much of their lives have been forgotten or lost to history. Therefore, I began this fictional work with scripture as a framework and developed the story from there.

I acknowledge that much of this story is a fabrication in my imagination, but I found so much more in writing it. I was able to place my own life into the lives of those who lived long ago. Using my own real emotions, I created a story around how they could have responded to their experiences. For instance, while writing about Cain's jealousy, anger, and subsequent irreversible actions, I found these were experiences I could unpack with my own emotions in similar moments. It was the same for the joys I unpacked in this book. These ways I have written are expressions of the joys that I have felt. When Eagle is soaring and doing the things he was designed to do, I could connect with moments when I was living out my own design. This has become a cathartic experience for me.

So, an idea that began in one way has finished in a totally different way. One chapter led to another, and before I knew it, a complete book had flowed out, and I was only up to Genesis 5!

The experience of writing a book like this has blessed me in ways that are difficult to explain. I discovered putting my own emotions into the biblical characters opened up a new paradigm for me to understand God (aka the Designer) through. I have always believed Him to be a present and loving God, but this gave me the opportunity to slow my thinking down to understand how He feels pain, sadness, grief, disappointment, joy, peace, and love through His grace. I look forward to writing more about other bible stories in the future. Some of them have been traditionally difficult to find grace in, like Noah's great flood (my next book). In that story, all of humanity was wiped out by God. How could a God of love do this to His own creation? The question remained in my spirit, and I got curious. Then a quest formed to discover this present and loving God in ways I had not explored before.

One of the key areas my curiosity explored in *Three Trees* was the presence of a God. I think I had grown up believing the God we meet in Genesis 1 was a distant and far away God; those days are gone. It was the phrase 'walked with them in the cool of the evening' in Genesis 3 that caught my imagination and piqued my curiosity for what that means for me now. From what I've learned through the bible and my personal experiences, I now believe in a present and loving God; where He surrounds me, and there is nowhere I can go to escape him. As I sat with this verse and these thoughts, I started writing, and very quickly, my mind formed the narrative of a God who walked with them and would never abandon them, a narrative I know is true for my own life. I know I am thousands of years outside of this time, but at the same time, I believe His love for me is as real as His love for Adam and Eve.

I believe there is far more revelation of God's character to come through the creativity of my writing.

I would also like to address some of my conclusions through writing this story. For those familiar with the Bible account of Genesis 1–5, you will notice that placing Cain and Abel in Eden before Eve eats the fruit may be a problem chronologically and scripturally. I agree that this is the case; however, I chose to put them in Eden as I wanted to express the generational challenges that happen when a parent does something that affects their children. It was by no fault of Cain or Abel that they were taken from Eden, but it would have affected their lives greatly. They wouldn't have understood the loss, guilt, or shame that Adam and Eve felt, which would have likely challenged their daily lives. These emotional challenges affect all people, and having Cain and Abel in Eden allows me to express how much life has changed for them.

I also believe the time Adam and Eve spent in Eden was far longer than what has been traditionally believed and taught. As you will see in Chapter 1, I have placed this into a concept of many years, and I find it hard to believe that children wouldn't have resulted from Adam and Eve's oneness and design to reproduce.

I have also taken apart a few other traditionally held concepts around the sacrificial system that Genesis attributed to Abel and Cain. As we have no idea when or how this started, I felt it would be helpful to take a look at the Hebrew word for 'sacrifice', which can be translated as 'gift.' So, I shifted from a lamb that needed to die or grain that needed to be burnt for the Designer to receive it or to receive his pleasure and had Him present. As a gift, I could have the Designer appraise the wonder of His own goodness in the gifts and return them to the people. To me, this seemed to flow powerfully with how His creation works and sustains itself. For me, it also worked with the concept that God was with the people and not distant from them. There are other moments in the Old and New Testaments where this holds true, like when Gideon prepares a meal for the Angel of the Lord or when Jesus eats with his disciples after his resurrection.

Abel's wife, Miriam, is a work of fiction, as is the child she would bear. Miriam, in Hebrew, can be translated 'wish for a child.' There is no record of Abel's children, but it would make sense that he may have had children. I believe the time between leaving Eden and Abel's death would have been many years, and by that time, more and more people were starting to appear.

As to how they appeared, this is a source of great question. Genesis chapter 1 shows that God created far more than Adam and Eve, and genesis chapter 5 would seem to back that up. Whereas Genesis 2 has creation of humans centered specifically on Adam and Eve. In my own experience, the latter has generally been taught at the cost of the former, but I hope you give me some grace to believe that the Designer might have been creating more people than just Adam and Eve. This also makes more sense of Cain finding a wife and having his own children.

Speaking of Cain's children, Enoch is one of Cain's sons, as recorded in Genesis 4, but he is not the Enoch that is born in Seth's line who would eventually become Noah's great-grandfather.

By placing Cain's Enoch where I did, I was simply building Cain's character around the concept that he was doing everything in his own strength and needed no one else, not even his own family.

I also took the liberty of placing Abel's funeral in Eden as well. I know there is nothing documented about this, but there was something about the bible's recount of Abel's blood calling to God from the ground that gave me the inspiration to bring Abel back to the ground of Eden.

You will also note how I've allowed for the potential of Adam and Eve to reconnect with Cain. It would be hard for me to believe they never met again because they lived for so long. Although they apparently lived a long distance from each other, hundreds of years is a long time to avoid one another. As a parent, I can easily see the case for Adam and Eve reconnecting with Cain, especially as the bible records the city that Cain built, which meant they knew where he lived and that he was not so far away that the journey would be impossible.

The Bible also doesn't record the deaths of Adam, Eve, or Cain, so there is no reason for me to believe God would have turned His back on any of them. As you can see from the book, I have adopted a belief Jesus is the same yesterday, today, and forever. Which, to me, means that God's character is the same regardless of the time period. With this being the case, I have written from the belief that He is love and has always been love. The overarching principle of this was the same for Cain as it is for me. If Jesus would leave the ninety-nine to find the lost sheep, then I believe he would have done the same for Cain and brought him back rejoicing.

Also, it has been traditionally taught that God used Cain as an example to show what would happen to one who did not listen to Him. While I understand this, I simply cannot agree with it. To agree with it would lead me to believe this deed of Cain's was beyond God's forgiveness and outside His grace. This most definitely wasn't the case for others in scripture who would also do the same thing as Cain in murdering a man (Moses, Samson, David, and even Paul would have followed suit if that was the case).

The mark placed on Cain in scripture is something that I've always considered to have been so horrific it would keep people away from him due to seeing him as evil. People tend to avoid people who identify as evil. After much pondering on this, I decided this image does not fit a gracious God who is love. I believe God to be about restoration, and denying Cain the opportunity for restoration would go against His character. I don't believe God would be unfaithful to his character. So, when I came to write about this mark, it dawned on me that God's mercy marked Cain. He would become known for God's mercy and not as a murderer. Once he received His mercy, he no longer feared losing God's presence (which is my understanding of death).

I'm sure I made other assumptions in the story that aren't recorded here, and there are smarter people than I who know much more than I about this time in our history. But, for me, I have discovered that in sharing our stories, we see and share from our own experiences and interpret them through the lens through which we understand the world. This alone is why the Bible is such a valuable source of hearing God speak. No matter how often you read the same story, you often find new understandings or revelations of Him within them. They are new to us because we are experiencing events and emotions uniquely and differently every time we read them. Our experiences constantly change our lives. As we grow and change, so does God's voice and revelation of himself to us.

It has been a joy to write this, and I hope it has been helpful for you as you journey through this thing called life.

ARTIST NOTE

I have been a professional artist for nearly 20 years with a deep desire to bring the stories of the Bible to life in a way that we can see ourselves within the narratives. I have had the extraordinary honor of partnering my theological training with artistic endeavors, allowing me to discover the transformative power that creativity has within the kingdom of God.

Three Trees is a story full of striking metaphors and imagination that entices the senses and invites us into a place of awe and wonder. We soar with Eagle to discover intimacy with the Designer in ways we may have never imagined, and yet we get to see for ourselves as we journey through each page. As an artist, what struck me the most were the moments that we get to witness the love and presence of the Designer in relationship to His creation. Each time we are watching Eagle or Wisdom take flight, we are watching God's design unfold in all of its beauty before us as it works in perfect harmony. From the thermals in the mountaintops to the flowing waters of the Euphrates River, we step into the Designer's world with Him and the people He loves.

As I sat with the pages, I was fixed on the notion of ancient life and the world that Adam and Eve were a part of outside of Eden. The way they lived intimately connected to the world inspired a stylized approach to my paintings, where I stripped away form and the complexities of shading and volume to expose the simple art of line. These lines are intended to weave through each image as patterns and shapes, creating continuity like a thread. I wanted to explore the landscapes and the trees with the simple strokes of my brush, each one connected to the other through repetition and movement. Unity being the heartbeat and rhythm keeping everything together.

I've always been intrigued with the mathematical concept of line being something that has no beginning and no end, infinite by its nature. This to me, represents the Designer and His infinite love, a love that has no limits and is endless. This is the kind of love I can see present when the Designer led Adam and Eve away from Eden. I wanted to capture the tenderness of the moment through an image of the Designer holding onto Eve with both hands. A reminder that there are moments in life we may feel like we aren't holding on, but His endless love is always first and foremost, holding onto us with both hands held tight.

Another chapter where love seems to have no limits is the moment in the story where Abel brings his gift to the Designer and, as a shepherd, he brings his best forward. It reminds me of the song we sing at Christmas of the drummer boy and how he believes he has no gift that is fit to lie before the king. He then plays his drum, the gift that he has within himself as an offering. I wanted this to be a revealing moment of Abel's heart in the same sense. As he holds his gift close to his chest, he is showing us the way he gives from a place of pure love and not out of obligation. The same I imagine, when Abel meets with the Designer in the cool of the night on the river's edge. The silhouettes I've used in this painting series represent a moment that cannot be fully realized with our eyes as it is something that is only known through the experience of the ones fully present. It is also my intention to leave room for the imagination to wander into the scene with a hint of mystery.

One of the most powerful revelations I found that continually expanded throughout the narrative was the power of love that came when one could push through the pain and into the heart of the Designer Himself. Reaching deep into the soil, connecting to the life and the love that flows in and through all of creation, was something I wanted to capture with both Eagle and Cain. With Eagle, there is a sense of connection that came from a place of complete surrender and giving of himself to love. With Cain, I wanted to hold the tension of his past and his struggle to surrender by focusing only on a small portion of a much bigger story as he drives his hands into the earth. The same earth that his father was created from through the breath of life. The same earth that Cain was commissioned to work. The same earth that held his greatest regret and cried out his shame. The same earth that offered him healing and complete forgiveness. This is the power of the infinite love that knows no limits and has no beginning and no end.

One last image that I most often find myself coming back to is the Designer making a fire and sitting by its warmth as the flames burst forth, bringing light into the darkness. There is something in this moment with the Designer's divinity colliding with our humanity that brings me back to the incomprehensible gift it is to be made in the image of God. What would it look like to sit at a fire in the presence of the one who is the light of the world?

Thank you, Matt Beckenham, for writing this beautiful story of the greatest love the world has ever known and inviting me to bring this to life in a visual sense. My prayer is that the artwork will enhance the experience you have created for your readers as you guide them into a deeper place of encounter within the biblical stories that have captured our hearts for so long.

Jessie DeCorsey

ABOUT THE AUTHOR

Matt is an author, speaker, and teacher whose desire is to help people discover their identity and design. His work stretches out beyond the four walls of the church and is an invitation to explore the narrative of how a relationship with God moves and unfolds in our daily lives.

Matt, along with his wife, Trish, are the founders of Greater Things International, which draws people together from all over the world to deepen their relationship with God. With their 30 years of ministry and counseling, they are committed to seeing people live in the freedom of their original design through community and connection.

His desire is that everyone would discover the immense love of the Designer, and live from His design for us. Over the years, Matt has done this through each of his books, online courses, mentoring and the Greater Things International podcasts.

Matt was born in Australia where he and Trish currently live and have three adult children. Before stepping into Greater Things International, he was in pastoral ministry for 19 years.

Prior to this, he worked in structural and civil engineering as a draftsperson and IT Manager.

If he and Trish are not in Sydney, you'll often find them exploring New Zealand, a place that has captured their hearts. To be a part of this movement, you can find Matt at:

greaterthingsinternational.com

Winifred DeCorsey (age 6)

COMING SOON

An extract of Matt's next book

THREE FLOODS

PROLOGUE

Many years have gone by since my charge was to watch over Adam and Eve, who have now passed and joined Abel. From the ground, they were made, and to the ground, they returned. But the glow they contained could not be buried. Their spirits lived on and never tasted death.

Their youngest son, Seth, carried the glow of his family, for he also loved to walk in the cool of the evening with the Designer. He had a presence about him that showed he was confident and happy with who he was.

He loved people well and knew how to work the soil. Seth seemed to carry the best of both his older brothers, even though he had grown up without either of them being around. Before Seth was born, Abel had passed, and Cain had moved away to build the city of Enoch.

That was a day that continues to be in my thoughts as if it had just happened. I still remember so clearly when Enoch, Cain's son, defied his father and brought the best gift possible from his harvest. I even find myself smiling when I remember Cain's shocked face and his son carried the glow of the Designer.

However, what followed from that continues to be in my mind as if it were yesterday. I can still see Abel's blood on the ground with Cain's digging tool lying in it. Oh, then there were the screams of Miriam and Eve as they realized what had happened.

Long after Abel's death, I would often find Eve sitting on the ground where his body had laid. She would be there for hours, and no one dared disturb her. Sometimes she would return home with tears in her eyes, and at other times, she'd come home telling anyone who would listen of all the things Abel had achieved. Eve ensured Abel's memory never faded.

The Designer had marked Cain with his mercy so many years ago, a mark he carried for the rest of his life. He went on and built the magnificent city of Enoch, named after his son. It was a place where he could, once again, apply his ingenuity. Cain and his family thrived in that land.

People were drawn to this city for many reasons. It was prosperous, and many traveled long distances to trade there. The city became renowned for the tools its tradespeople would make. It also became renowned for the master craftsmen who created instruments, in particular, harps and flutes. The sounds that flowed from these instruments they called music. The sounds they made would move my soul. I could have sat and listened to them play until the end of my days.

But it was the many conversations with the tradespeople that excited Cain. He would sit with them for hours, locking minds around fixing a problem. Invariably after a long night of mind wrestling, they would emerge with a solution and a tool to help them.

But, the primary reason people would travel to the city of Enoch was to see the Designer's mark on Cain. The story of one brother killing the other had traveled to places near and far. It was a pain that Cain carried with him all the days of his life. The mark, however, took people's breath away when they saw it. The glow that came from Cain drew people to him, and they would often leave with the same glow. Many would talk about being healed or changed by being in Cain's presence.

Adam and Eve would often make the trip to the city of Enoch to see their son. Their first trip was challenging, as it was the first time they had seen Cain since he fled. The Designer went with them. I remember He invited the three of them to sit with Him on the ground to place their hands into the dirt to feel the love flowing into them all. Many tears were shed on that trip. As each trip came and went, it became less challenging, but I don't know if it ever became easy. Some wounds seem to take a lifetime to heal.

Miriam and Abel's baby was born a few months after Abel's death, and he was a fine young boy. His mother gave him the name of his father. The name Abel means His Breath, and it is a beautiful name to hear. Hearing Miriam call his name was like listening to the Designer speak Adam into existence all those years ago. Abel was breathed into again. Miriam was so proud to call him Abel. He grew to be a shepherd like his father. The lessons his father had taught to his apprentices were passed to his son, and he was a fast learner.

Once Adam and Eve had passed, the Designer charged me to watch over Seth. Generations of faithful people would come from Seth. But it was to his son, Enosh; the Designer revealed one of His names. I had only ever known Him as "the Designer" or called Him "my Lord." To discover He had a name shocked me at first. But when he spoke it, it was like I had known it all along: He became known as Yahweh, which means He brings into existence whatever exists.

The atmosphere would shift whenever someone spoke Yahweh. It was a powerful name that inspired awe. The Designer loved His name and loved to share His presence and His love with His people. What had started with Adam and Eve walking in the cool of the evening with Him became a crowd of their family gathering by the banks of the Tigris River each evening. It was a beautiful time for everyone there. They would wait on every word that He spoke. They would sit and feel the powerful love that holds everything together, flowing through the ground.

Over time, though, the people spoke His name out loud less and less. Some claimed that it was too awe-inspiring to come from the lips of people who had given up Eden. One day when I asked the Designer about this, I could see His countenance change.

He said, "They are beginning to believe more in my name than in who I am." He was silent for a time before He continued, "My name is indeed all they have described, but it is who I am that I long for them to see and connect with. It is not a word that merely defines me; it is a word that invites me."

He continued, "I have never stopped inviting people to sit with me, as Adam and Eve once did. You saw this many times, Eagle. You were there when they would walk home glowing after being with me. They had been permitted to understand the mysteries of my kingdom. They called me 'friend', just like I have called you 'friend'. The glow you saw in them is not because I favor or love them any more than anyone in my creation. They are the ones who have learned I love to walk with them. I would walk with any of the people I have created, but I will not force them to walk with me. In here, Eagle is the essence of the invitation of my name."

That was many years ago, and I have had many charges to watch over. I would watch the Designer love them as He loved all of His creation. His character remained as true as His love. To each, He gave the freedom to choose Him or to leave Him. It was a choice He would always allow, even when it hurt Him terribly. For, He knew that if He withdrew their choice, He would have already withdrawn His love from them.

The Designer had commissioned me to watch over Seth's generational line. And now, my charge has changed again.

CHAPTER 1

Generations had come and gone. From Seth would come Enosh. From Enosh would come, Kenan. From Kenan would come Mahalael. From Mahalael would come Jared, and from Jared would come one another called Enoch.

Each generation had its own expression of relationship with the Designer. Since Seth and Enosh, few had carried the same intensity of glow, and rarely would I find people walking with the Designer in the cool of the evening. They would occasionally come, but difficult seasons usually marked these times. When there was not enough rain, they would go back to the banks of the Tigris and wait to meet with the Designer to ask for rain. Once the rains returned, people seemed to find other things to do rather than walk in the cool of the evening with the Designer.

That was until Enoch came along. He was at the river every evening and always glowed with the Designer's presence. It was not need that drew him to His presence; it was the Designer's love. I often wondered if it was reciprocal and if Enoch's love drew the Designer to him.

He loved to spend all of his time with the Designer. People would often make jests about him. They often called him 'The Designer's favorite' and mocked him, but it never bothered Enoch. It baffled him why everyone wasn't at the river each evening.

Both Wisdom and I loved spending time with Enoch. Wisdom would be found talking with him long into the night. They would share with each other the most astounding things; things I had never seen or heard of, about the future, and of angels I had never met. I loved listening to them.

Enoch was a person who saw glorious visions and had monumental dreams. Sometimes he would share what he saw with me, but it was often beyond my imagination to grasp all the realms and angelic forces he described. He spoke of great battles that were yet to happen, which mostly seemed to happen in the spiritual realm. But the way he shared them fascinated me, and I always longed for more.

Enoch lived within sight of Eden for three hundred years and was always close to the Designer's heart. As I said, he was often, if not always, by the banks of the Tigris River waiting for the Designer. It was a rare moment if the Designer arrived and Enoch was not there. Days, weeks, months, and years were spent in His presence.

But then, on one of those days, of one of those weeks, on one of those years, Enoch disappeared. People looked for him everywhere, but no one could find him. Some said he became a wanderer like Cain and just walked off, but I didn't believe that. The day he disappeared, I was out soaring and looking for him when Wisdom flew right up to me. She came up so fast that I got a surprise. She laughed as she knew she had caught me off guard. Few can, but Wisdom could always do that.

She said, "Eagle, what are you doing out here?"

"I'm looking for Enoch," I said. "The Designer commissioned me to watch over him, and I've lost him!"

At that, she laughed, "Eagle, you will not find him out here."

"Wisdom," I replied, "If you know where he is, you must tell me!"

Still, she laughed, "Where did you see him last?"

"He was with the Designer on the banks of the Tigris River last evening," I said.

"Yes, he was Eagle," she replied. "You didn't see him return home, did you?"

"Of course, he must be still with the Designer!" I exclaimed.

"In a way, Eagle," she said.

"In a way? What do you mean, Wisdom? Please stop talking in riddles! You sound like the Designer!" I exclaimed.

That caused her to laugh again, which caused me to get frustrated.

"Eagle," she said, "The Designer took him back to Eden."

It took me a moment to understand what she had said. And when it did makes sense, I didn't know what to do. I was too shocked even to form words, and I nearly forgot I was flying.

Finally, I blurted out, "He took him to Eden?"

"Yes, Eagle, he took him to Eden, and Enoch ate from the *Tree of Life*!"

To be continued ...

CPSIA information can be obtained
at www.ICGtesting.com
Printed in the USA
BVHW042312230423
662840BV00003B/6

9 780645 786804